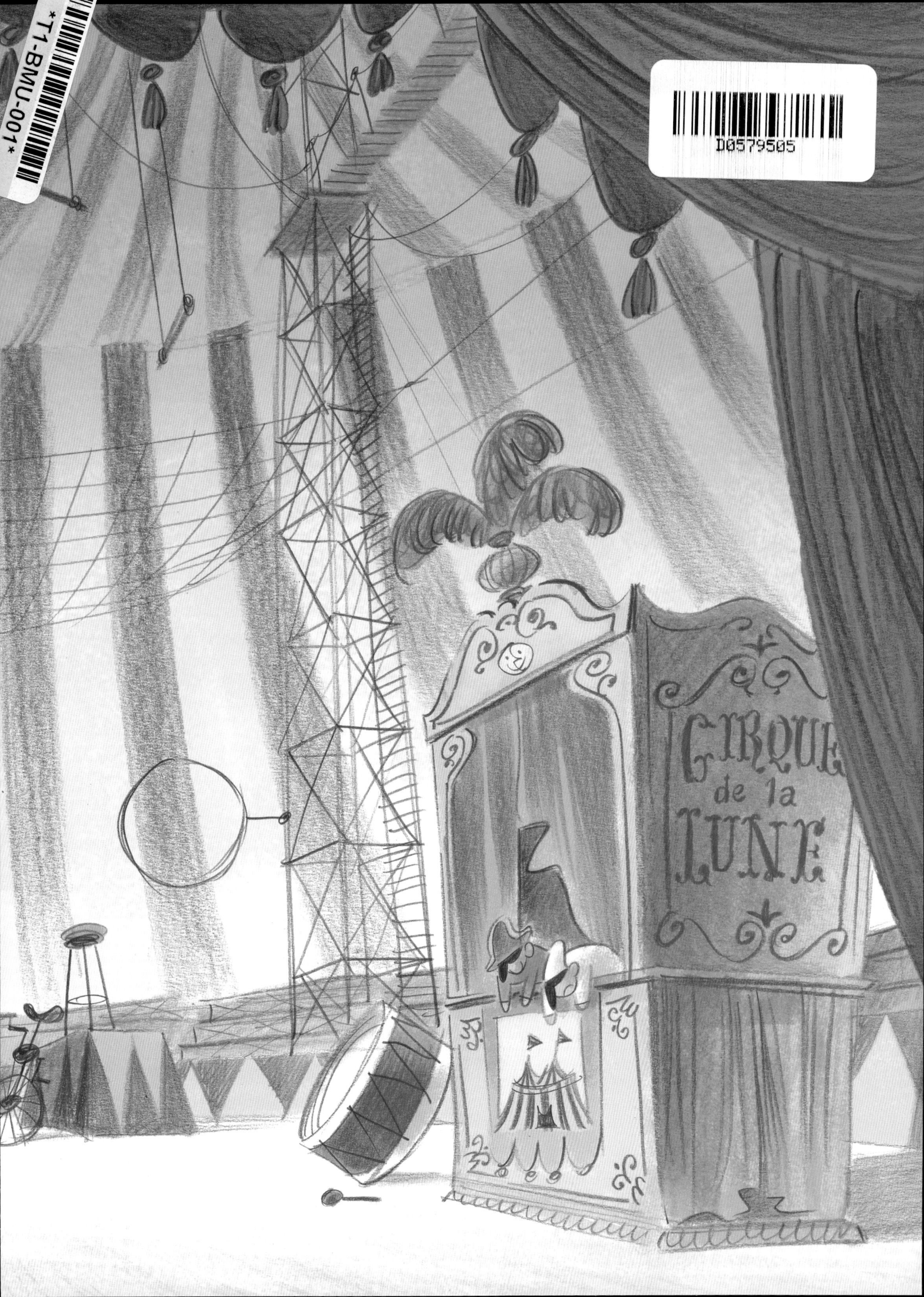
CIRQUE
de la
LUNE

"MAYBE MY HEAD IS OFTEN IN THE CLOUDS BECAUSE, LIKE THEM, I'M ALWAYS TRAVELING AND I DON'T KNOW WHERE THE WIND WILL TAKE ME..."

"MY NAME IS VIOLETTE VERMEER -- DUTCH FATHER, FRENCH MOTHER... CITIZEN OF THE WORLD!"

)ICE ★ STEFANO TURCONI

Violette
around the world

2. A New World Symphony

EURO COMICS
ENGLISH EDITION   GRAPHIC NOVELS
An imprint of IDW Publishing

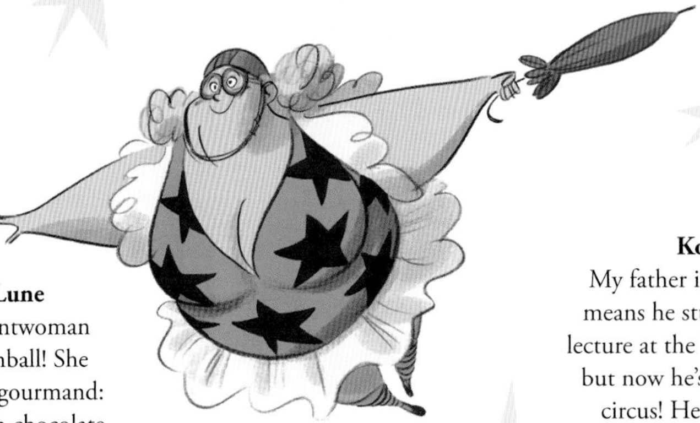

Amélie de la Lune
My mother is a stuntwoman and human cannonball! She is super sweet and a gourmand: she loves waffles with chocolate on top! She also sews beautiful patchwork quilts for people she likes.

Konrad Vermeer
My father is an entomologist. That means he studies insects! He used to lecture at the University of Amsterdam, but now he's the insect trainer in the circus! He always has his head in the clouds. (Which must be where I get it from!)

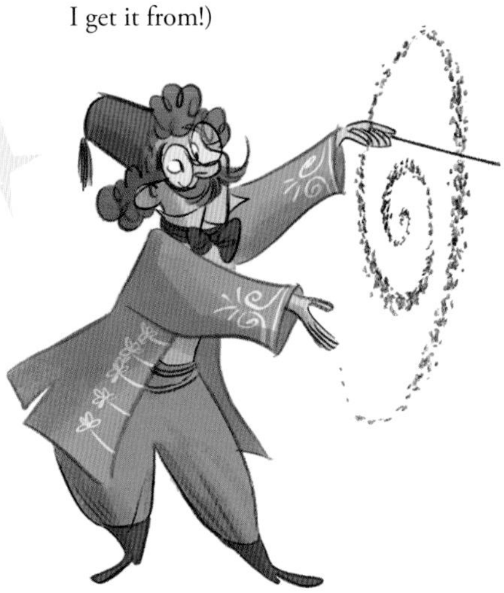

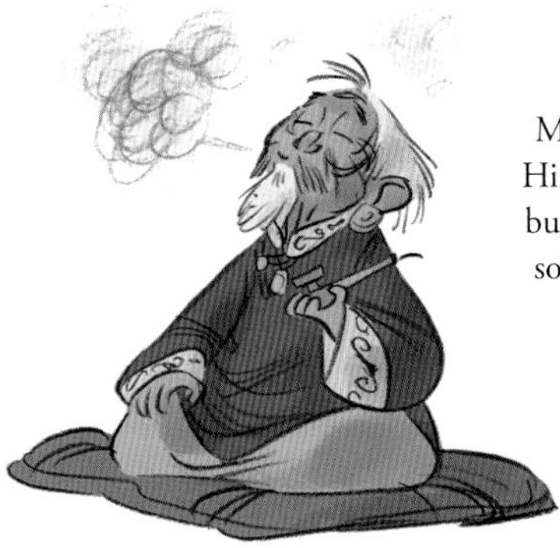

Grandad Tenzin
My grandfather was born in the Himalayas. He doesn't talk much, but when he does, it really means something. He is a great teacher and has infinite patience. He's a wise man!

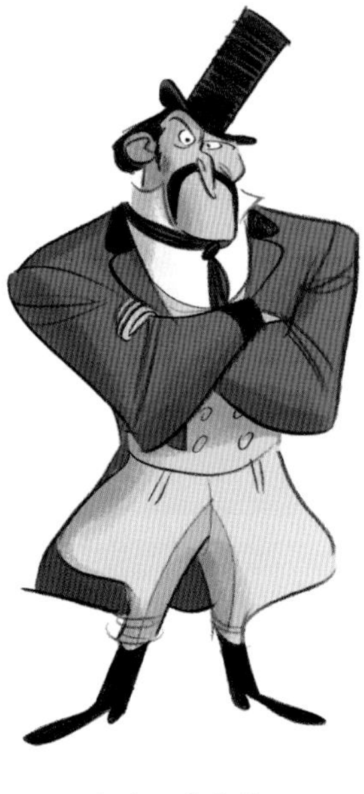

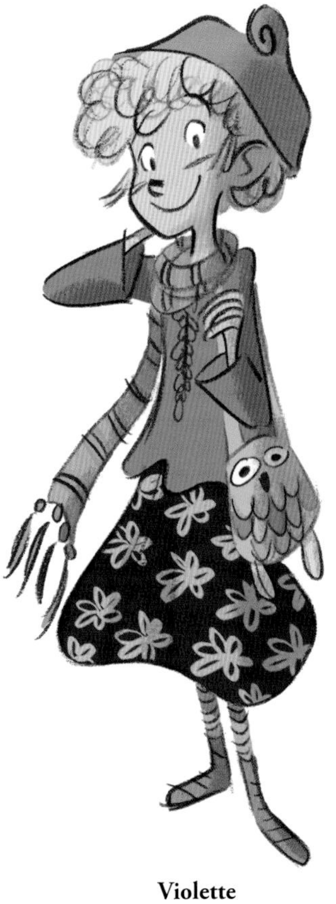

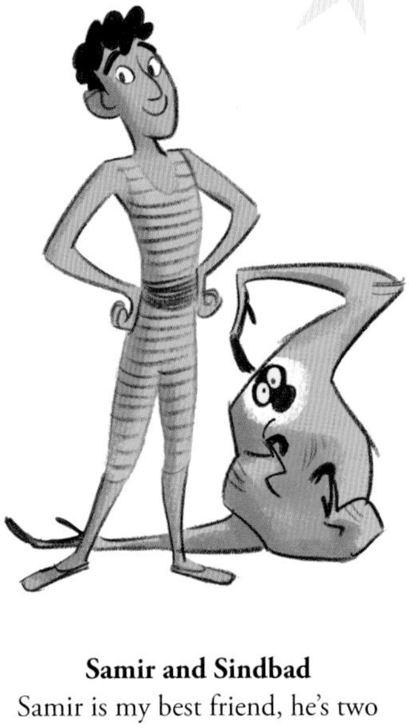

Samir and Sindbad
Samir is my best friend, he's two years older than me and he's a trapeze artist, like his big sister Fatima. They come from Damascus, just like Sindbad, their gibbon who follows Samir everywhere he goes!

Arsène de la Lune
Ah! My uncle Arsène! He looks grumpy, doesn't he? He's the director of our circus. When it comes down to it, though (and I swear to it!), he has a heart of gold.

Violette
...and here I am, Violette Vermeer, almost twelve years old. I love to travel and I'm curious about everything, always looking for the beauty in the world.

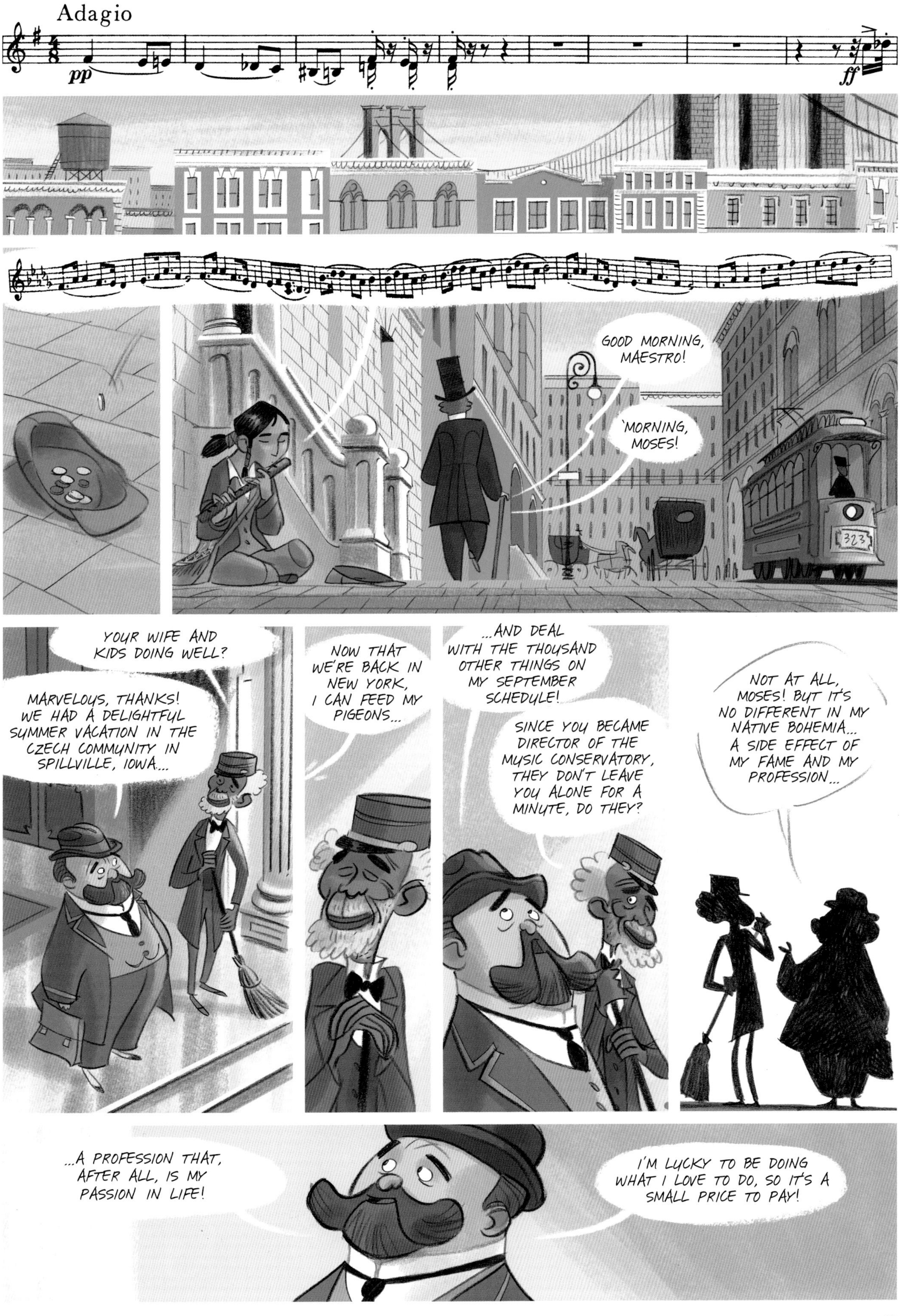
Adagio
pp
ff
GOOD MORNING, MAESTRO!
'MORNING, MOSES!
323
YOUR WIFE AND KIDS DOING WELL?
MARVELOUS, THANKS! WE HAD A DELIGHTFUL SUMMER VACATION IN THE CZECH COMMUNITY IN SPILLVILLE, IOWA...
NOW THAT WE'RE BACK IN NEW YORK, I CAN FEED MY PIGEONS...
...AND DEAL WITH THE THOUSAND OTHER THINGS ON MY SEPTEMBER SCHEDULE!
SINCE YOU BECAME DIRECTOR OF THE MUSIC CONSERVATORY, THEY DON'T LEAVE YOU ALONE FOR A MINUTE, DO THEY?
NOT AT ALL, MOSES! BUT IT'S NO DIFFERENT IN MY NATIVE BOHEMIA... A SIDE EFFECT OF MY FAME AND MY PROFESSION...
...A PROFESSION THAT, AFTER ALL, IS MY PASSION IN LIFE!
I'M LUCKY TO BE DOING WHAT I LOVE TO DO, SO IT'S A SMALL PRICE TO PAY!

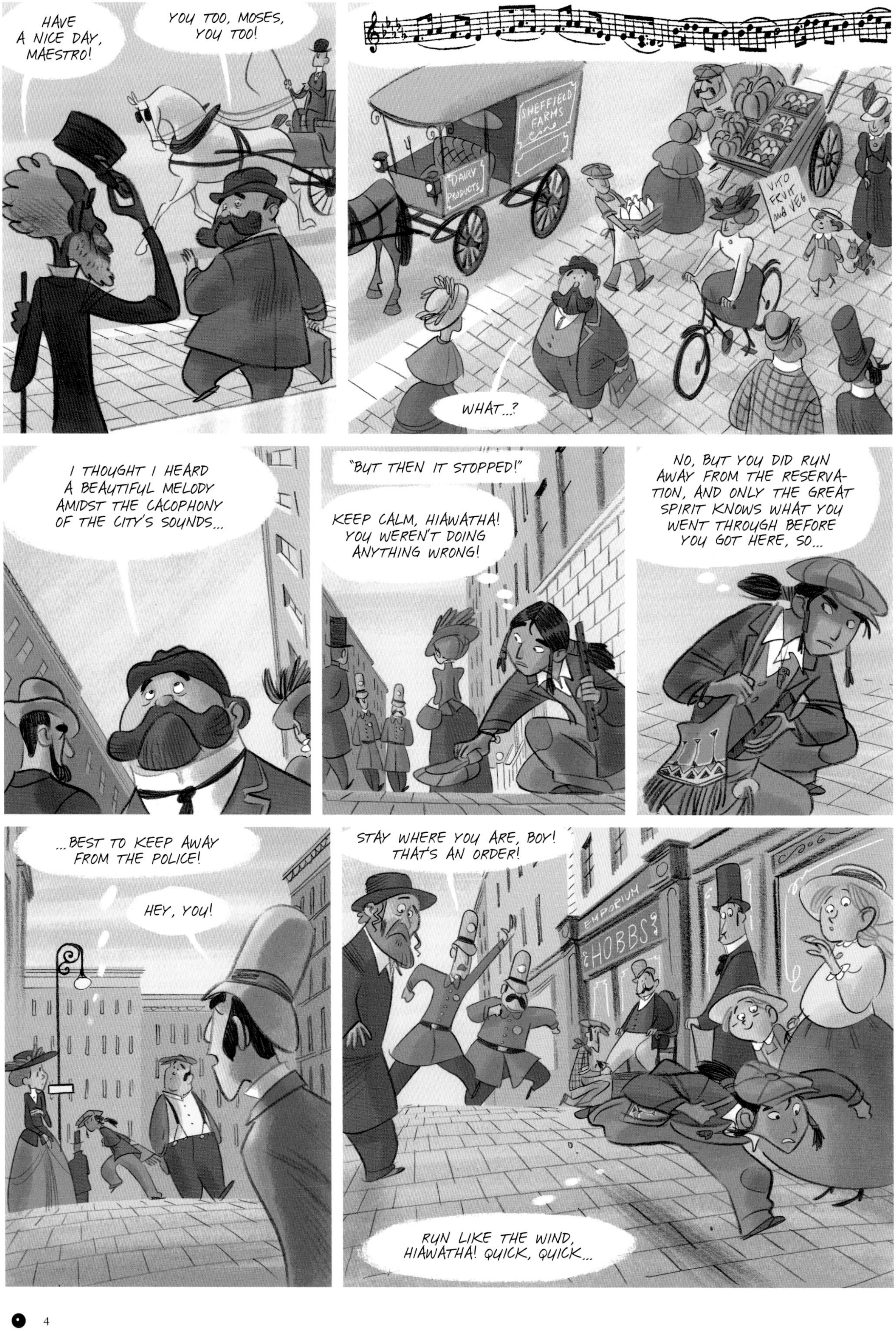
HAVE A NICE DAY, MAESTRO!
YOU TOO, MOSES, YOU TOO!
SHEFFIELD FARMS
DAIRY PRODUCTS
VITO FRUIT and VEG
WHAT...?
I THOUGHT I HEARD A BEAUTIFUL MELODY AMIDST THE CACOPHONY OF THE CITY'S SOUNDS...
"BUT THEN IT STOPPED!"
KEEP CALM, HIAWATHA! YOU WEREN'T DOING ANYTHING WRONG!
NO, BUT YOU DID RUN AWAY FROM THE RESERVATION, AND ONLY THE GREAT SPIRIT KNOWS WHAT YOU WENT THROUGH BEFORE YOU GOT HERE, SO...
...BEST TO KEEP AWAY FROM THE POLICE!
HEY, YOU!
STAY WHERE YOU ARE, BOY! THAT'S AN ORDER!
EMPORIUM
HOBBS
RUN LIKE THE WIND, HIAWATHA! QUICK, QUICK...

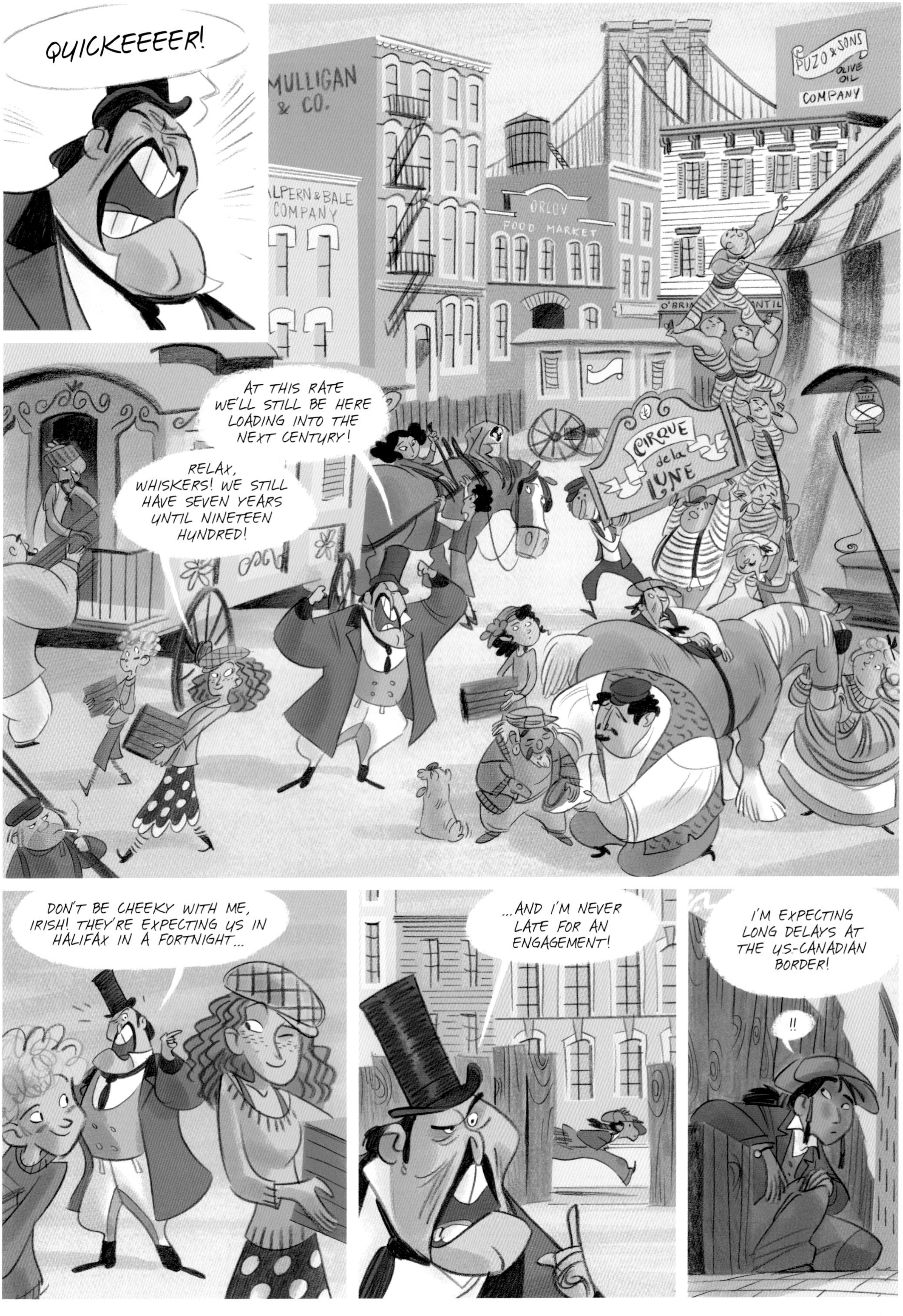
QUICKEEEER!
MULLIGAN & CO.
ALPERN & BALE COMPANY
ORLOV FOOD MARKET
PUZO & SONS OLIVE OIL COMPANY
CIRQUE de la LUNE
AT THIS RATE WE'LL STILL BE HERE LOADING INTO THE NEXT CENTURY!
RELAX, WHISKERS! WE STILL HAVE SEVEN YEARS UNTIL NINETEEN HUNDRED!
DON'T BE CHEEKY WITH ME, IRISH! THEY'RE EXPECTING US IN HALIFAX IN A FORTNIGHT...
...AND I'M NEVER LATE FOR AN ENGAGEMENT!
I'M EXPECTING LONG DELAYS AT THE U.S.-CANADIAN BORDER!
!!

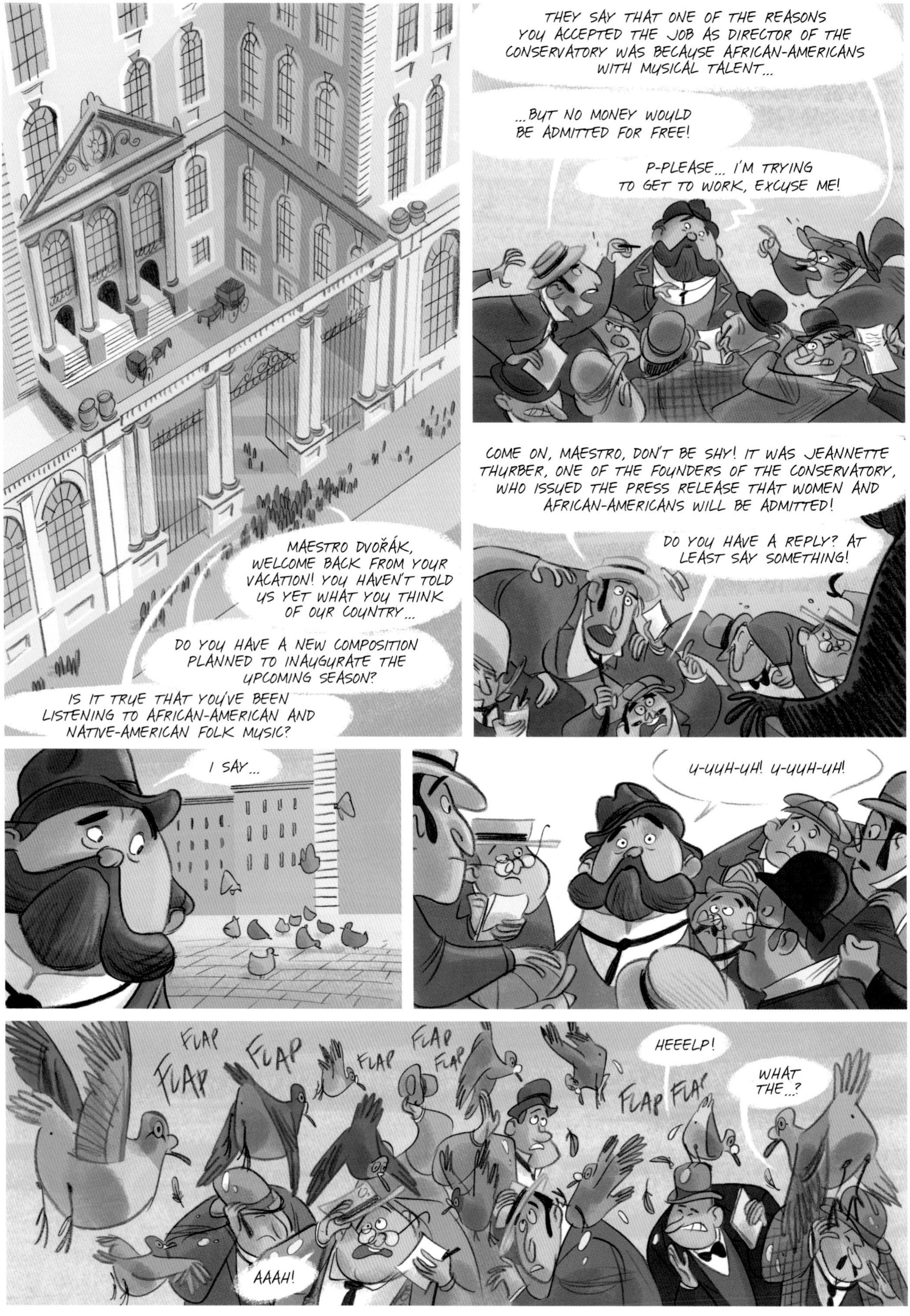
MAESTRO DVOŘÁK, WELCOME BACK FROM YOUR VACATION! YOU HAVEN'T TOLD US YET WHAT YOU THINK OF OUR COUNTRY...
DO YOU HAVE A NEW COMPOSITION PLANNED TO INAUGURATE THE UPCOMING SEASON?
IS IT TRUE THAT YOU'VE BEEN LISTENING TO AFRICAN-AMERICAN AND NATIVE-AMERICAN FOLK MUSIC?
THEY SAY THAT ONE OF THE REASONS YOU ACCEPTED THE JOB AS DIRECTOR OF THE CONSERVATORY WAS BECAUSE AFRICAN-AMERICANS WITH MUSICAL TALENT...
...BUT NO MONEY WOULD BE ADMITTED FOR FREE!
P-PLEASE... I'M TRYING TO GET TO WORK, EXCUSE ME!
COME ON, MAESTRO, DON'T BE SHY! IT WAS JEANNETTE THURBER, ONE OF THE FOUNDERS OF THE CONSERVATORY, WHO ISSUED THE PRESS RELEASE THAT WOMEN AND AFRICAN-AMERICANS WILL BE ADMITTED!
DO YOU HAVE A REPLY? AT LEAST SAY SOMETHING!
I SAY...
U-UUH-UH! U-UUH-UH!
FLAP FLAP FLAP FLAP FLAP FLAP
HEEELP!
FLAP FLAP
WHAT THE...?
AAAH!

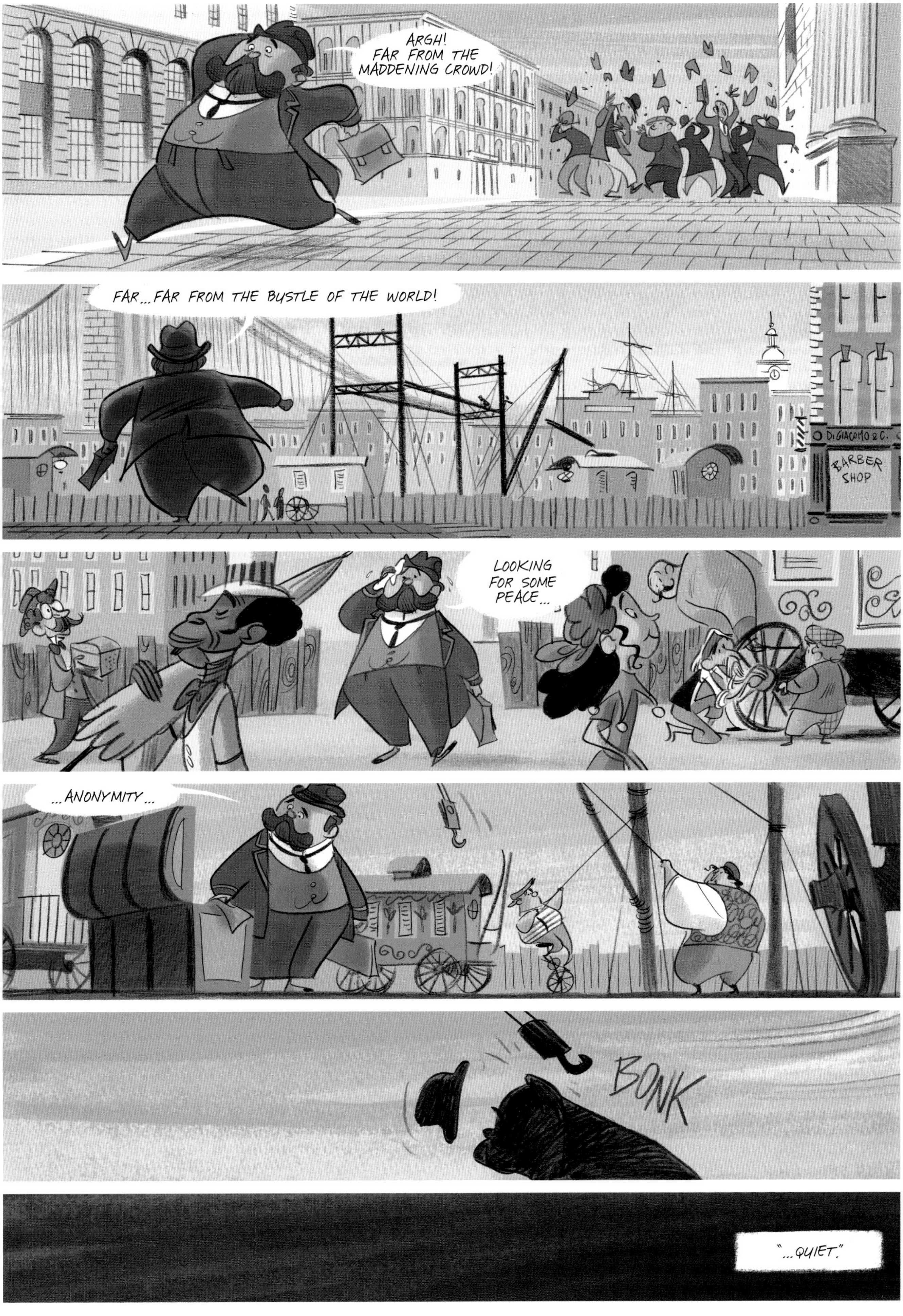
ARGH!
FAR FROM THE MADDENING CROWD!
FAR... FAR FROM THE BUSTLE OF THE WORLD!
DI GIACOMO & C.
BARBER SHOP
LOOKING FOR SOME PEACE...
...ANONYMITY...
BONK
"...QUIET."

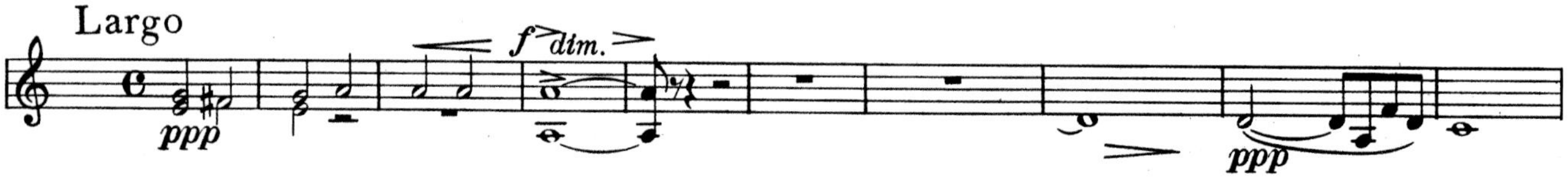
Largo
f dim.
ppp
ppp

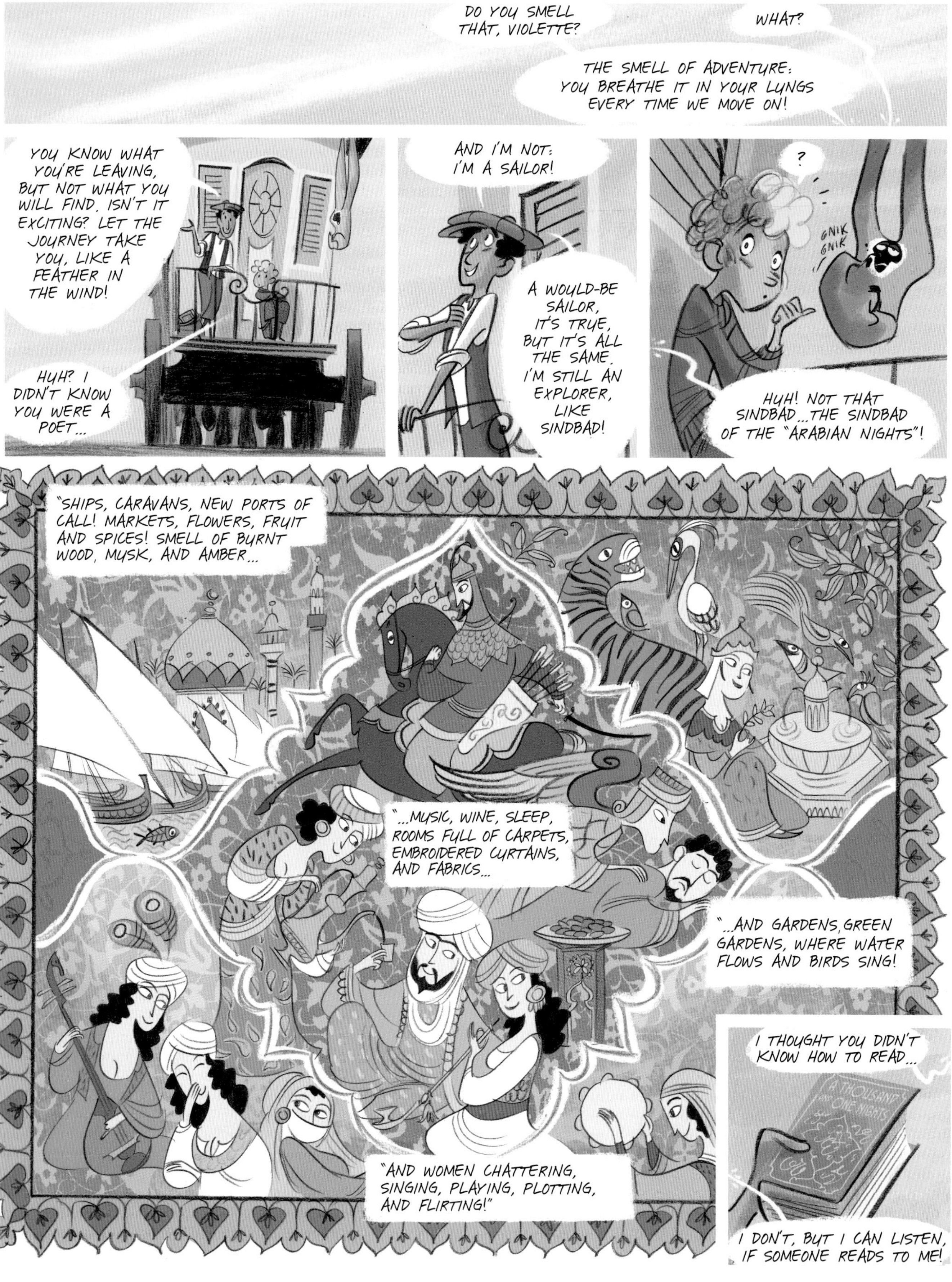
DO YOU SMELL THAT, VIOLETTE?
WHAT?
THE SMELL OF ADVENTURE: YOU BREATHE IT IN YOUR LUNGS EVERY TIME WE MOVE ON!
YOU KNOW WHAT YOU'RE LEAVING, BUT NOT WHAT YOU WILL FIND. ISN'T IT EXCITING? LET THE JOURNEY TAKE YOU, LIKE A FEATHER IN THE WIND!
HUH? I DIDN'T KNOW YOU WERE A POET...
AND I'M NOT: I'M A SAILOR!
A WOULD-BE SAILOR, IT'S TRUE, BUT IT'S ALL THE SAME. I'M STILL AN EXPLORER, LIKE SINDBAD!
?
GNIK GNIK
HUH! NOT THAT SINDBAD... THE SINDBAD OF THE "ARABIAN NIGHTS"!
"SHIPS, CARAVANS, NEW PORTS OF CALL! MARKETS, FLOWERS, FRUIT AND SPICES! SMELL OF BURNT WOOD, MUSK, AND AMBER...
"...MUSIC, WINE, SLEEP, ROOMS FULL OF CARPETS, EMBROIDERED CURTAINS, AND FABRICS...
"...AND GARDENS, GREEN GARDENS, WHERE WATER FLOWS AND BIRDS SING!
"AND WOMEN CHATTERING, SINGING, PLAYING, PLOTTING, AND FLIRTING!"
I THOUGHT YOU DIDN'T KNOW HOW TO READ...
A THOUSAND AND ONE NIGHTS
I DON'T, BUT I CAN LISTEN, IF SOMEONE READS TO ME!

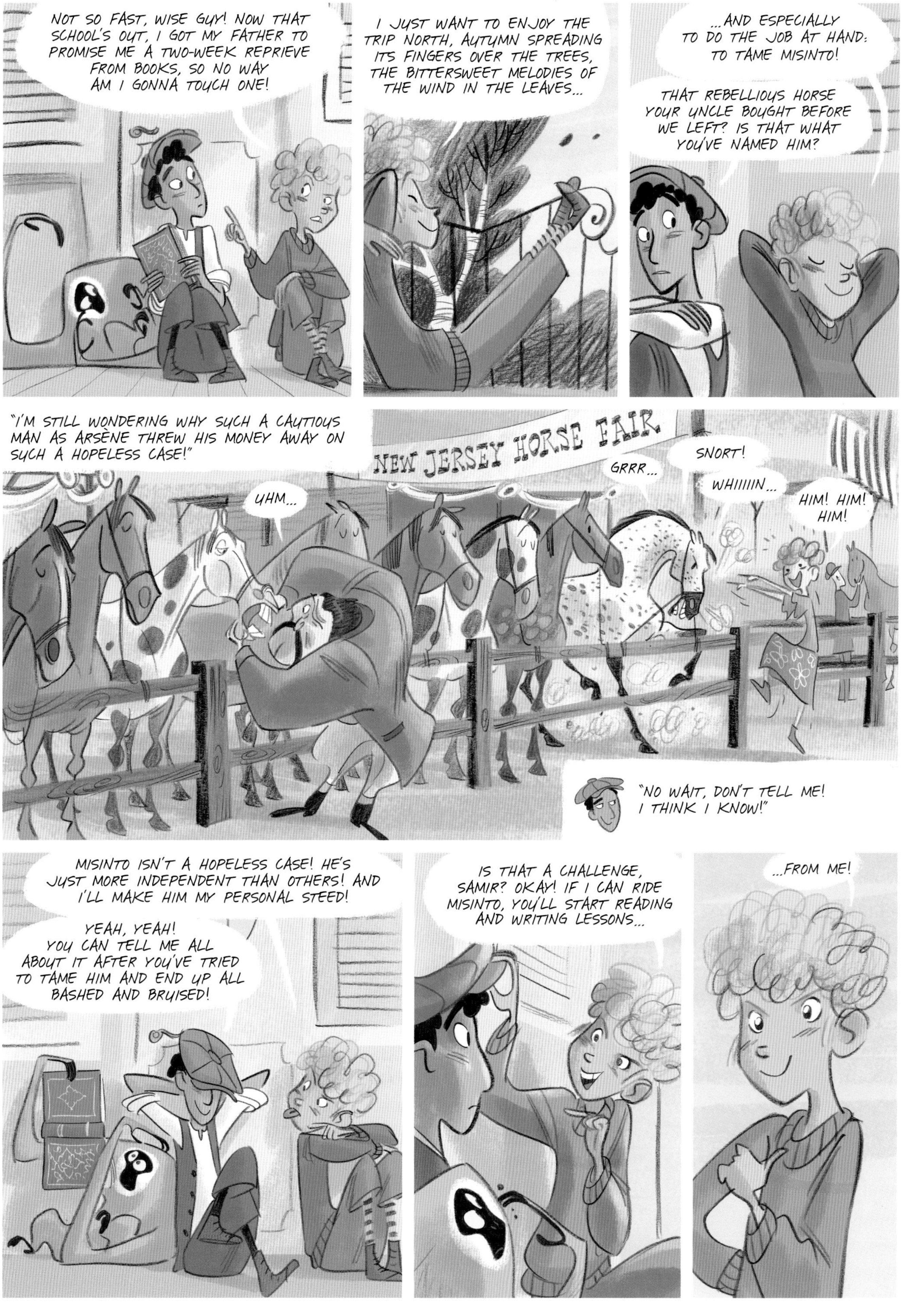
NOT SO FAST, WISE GUY! NOW THAT SCHOOL'S OUT, I GOT MY FATHER TO PROMISE ME A TWO-WEEK REPRIEVE FROM BOOKS, SO NO WAY AM I GONNA TOUCH ONE!
I JUST WANT TO ENJOY THE TRIP NORTH, AUTUMN SPREADING ITS FINGERS OVER THE TREES, THE BITTERSWEET MELODIES OF THE WIND IN THE LEAVES...
...AND ESPECIALLY TO DO THE JOB AT HAND: TO TAME MISINTO!
THAT REBELLIOUS HORSE YOUR UNCLE BOUGHT BEFORE WE LEFT? IS THAT WHAT YOU'VE NAMED HIM?
"I'M STILL WONDERING WHY SUCH A CAUTIOUS MAN AS ARSÈNE THREW HIS MONEY AWAY ON SUCH A HOPELESS CASE!"
NEW JERSEY HORSE FAIR
UHM...
GRRR...
SNORT!
WHIIIIIN...
HIM! HIM! HIM!
"NO WAIT, DON'T TELL ME! I THINK I KNOW!"
MISINTO ISN'T A HOPELESS CASE! HE'S JUST MORE INDEPENDENT THAN OTHERS! AND I'LL MAKE HIM MY PERSONAL STEED!
YEAH, YEAH! YOU CAN TELL ME ALL ABOUT IT AFTER YOU'VE TRIED TO TAME HIM AND END UP ALL BASHED AND BRUISED!
IS THAT A CHALLENGE, SAMIR? OKAY! IF I CAN RIDE MISINTO, YOU'LL START READING AND WRITING LESSONS...
...FROM ME!

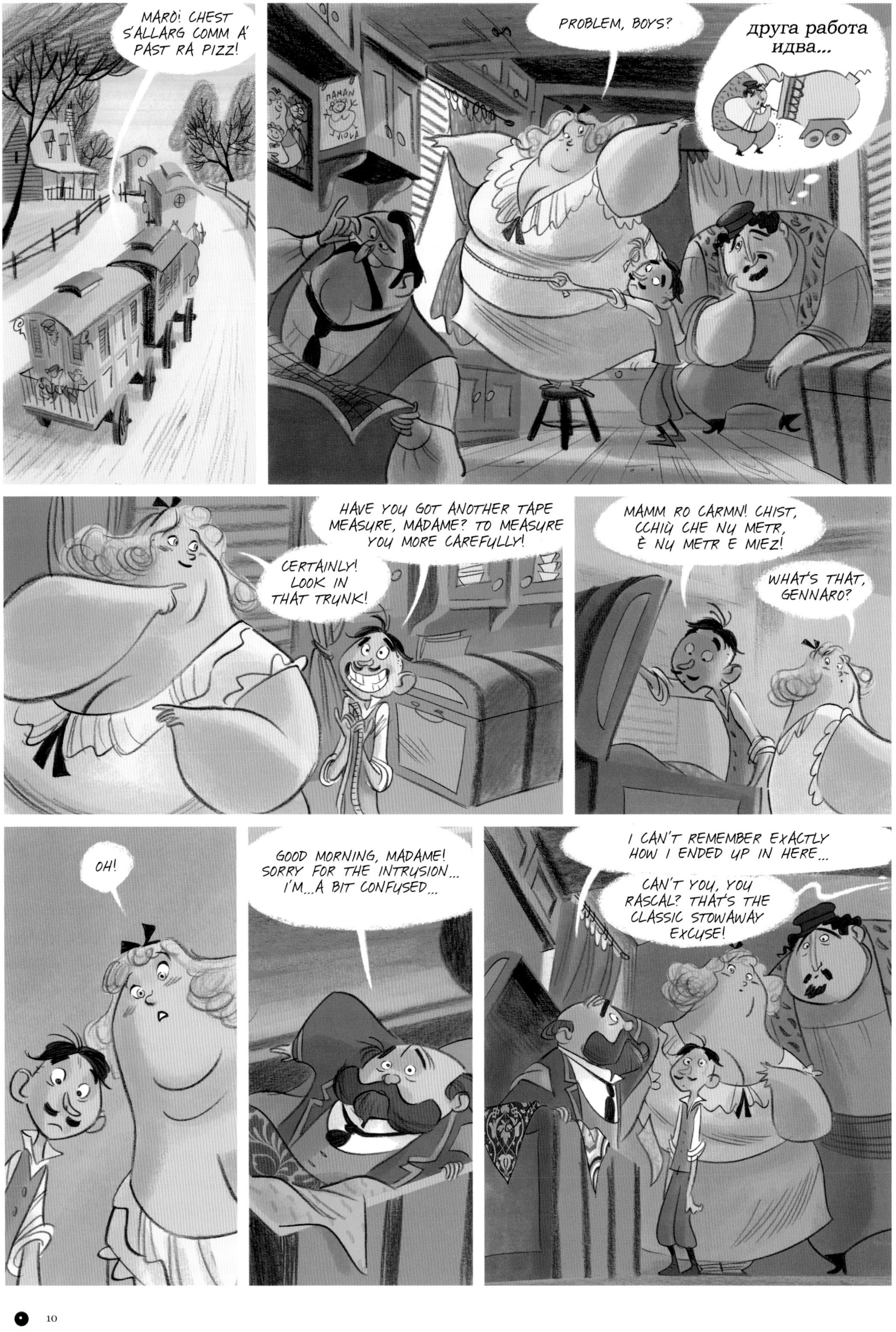
MARÒ! CHEST S'ALLARG COMM A' PAST RA PIZZ!
PROBLEM, BOYS?
MAMAN VIOLA
друга работа идва...
HAVE YOU GOT ANOTHER TAPE MEASURE, MADAME? TO MEASURE YOU MORE CAREFULLY!
CERTAINLY! LOOK IN THAT TRUNK!
MAMM RO CARMN! CHIST, CCHIÙ CHE NU METR, È NU METR E MIEZ!
WHAT'S THAT, GENNARO?
OH!
GOOD MORNING, MADAME! SORRY FOR THE INTRUSION... I'M...A BIT CONFUSED...
I CAN'T REMEMBER EXACTLY HOW I ENDED UP IN HERE...
CAN'T YOU, YOU RASCAL? THAT'S THE CLASSIC STOWAWAY EXCUSE!

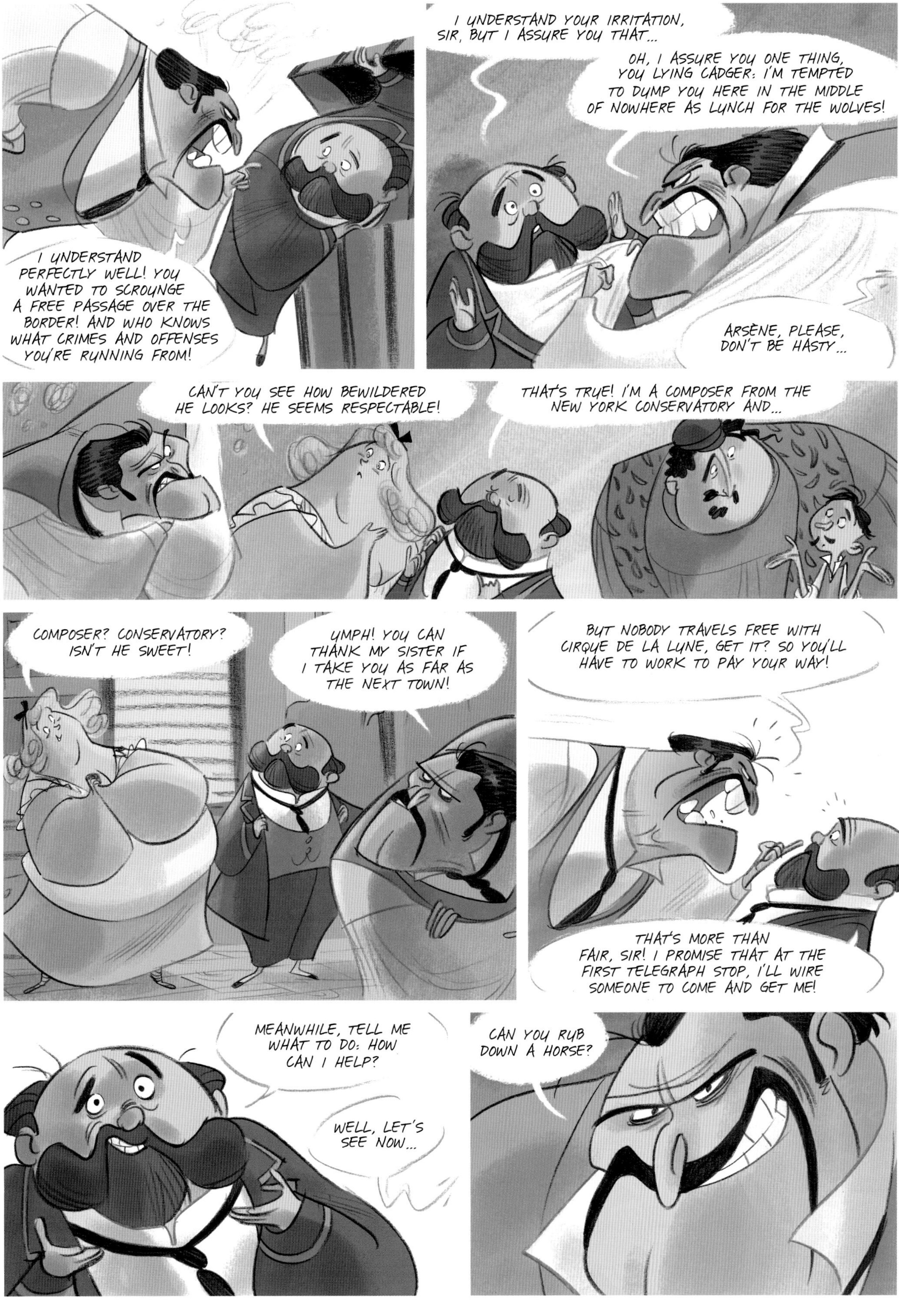
I UNDERSTAND PERFECTLY WELL! YOU WANTED TO SCROUNGE A FREE PASSAGE OVER THE BORDER! AND WHO KNOWS WHAT CRIMES AND OFFENSES YOU'RE RUNNING FROM!
I UNDERSTAND YOUR IRRITATION, SIR, BUT I ASSURE YOU THAT...
OH, I ASSURE YOU ONE THING, YOU LYING CADGER: I'M TEMPTED TO DUMP YOU HERE IN THE MIDDLE OF NOWHERE AS LUNCH FOR THE WOLVES!
ARSÈNE, PLEASE, DON'T BE HASTY...
CAN'T YOU SEE HOW BEWILDERED HE LOOKS? HE SEEMS RESPECTABLE!
THAT'S TRUE! I'M A COMPOSER FROM THE NEW YORK CONSERVATORY AND...
COMPOSER? CONSERVATORY? ISN'T HE SWEET!
UMPH! YOU CAN THANK MY SISTER IF I TAKE YOU AS FAR AS THE NEXT TOWN!
BUT NOBODY TRAVELS FREE WITH CIRQUE DE LA LUNE, GET IT? SO YOU'LL HAVE TO WORK TO PAY YOUR WAY!
THAT'S MORE THAN FAIR, SIR! I PROMISE THAT AT THE FIRST TELEGRAPH STOP, I'LL WIRE SOMEONE TO COME AND GET ME!
MEANWHILE, TELL ME WHAT TO DO: HOW CAN I HELP?
WELL, LET'S SEE NOW...
CAN YOU RUB DOWN A HORSE?

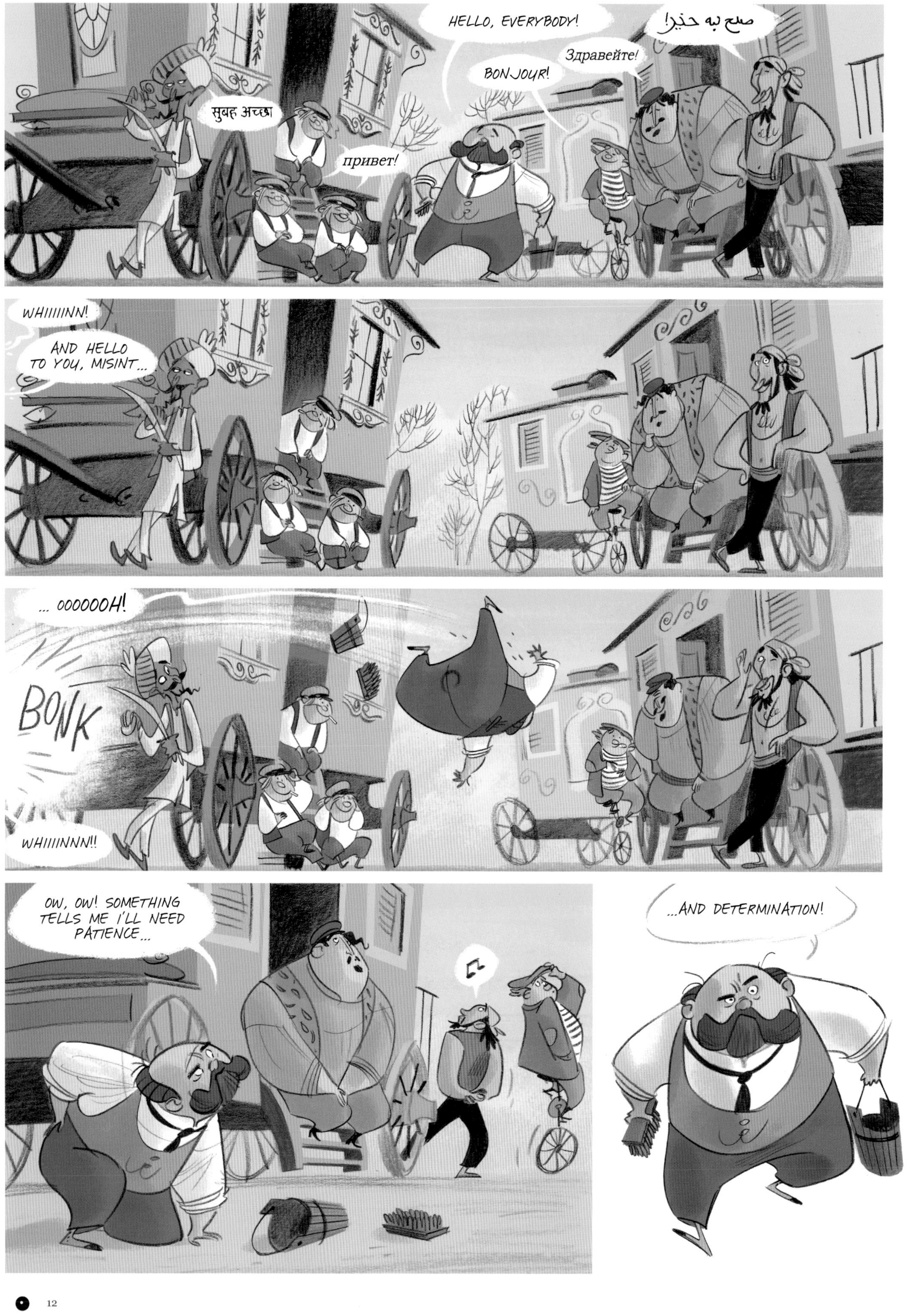
सुबह अच्छा
привет!
HELLO, EVERYBODY!
BONJOUR!
Здравейте!
صبح به خیر!
WHIIIIINN!
AND HELLO TO YOU, MISINT...
... OOOOOOH!
BONK
WHIIIINNN!!
OW, OW! SOMETHING TELLS ME I'LL NEED PATIENCE...
...AND DETERMINATION!

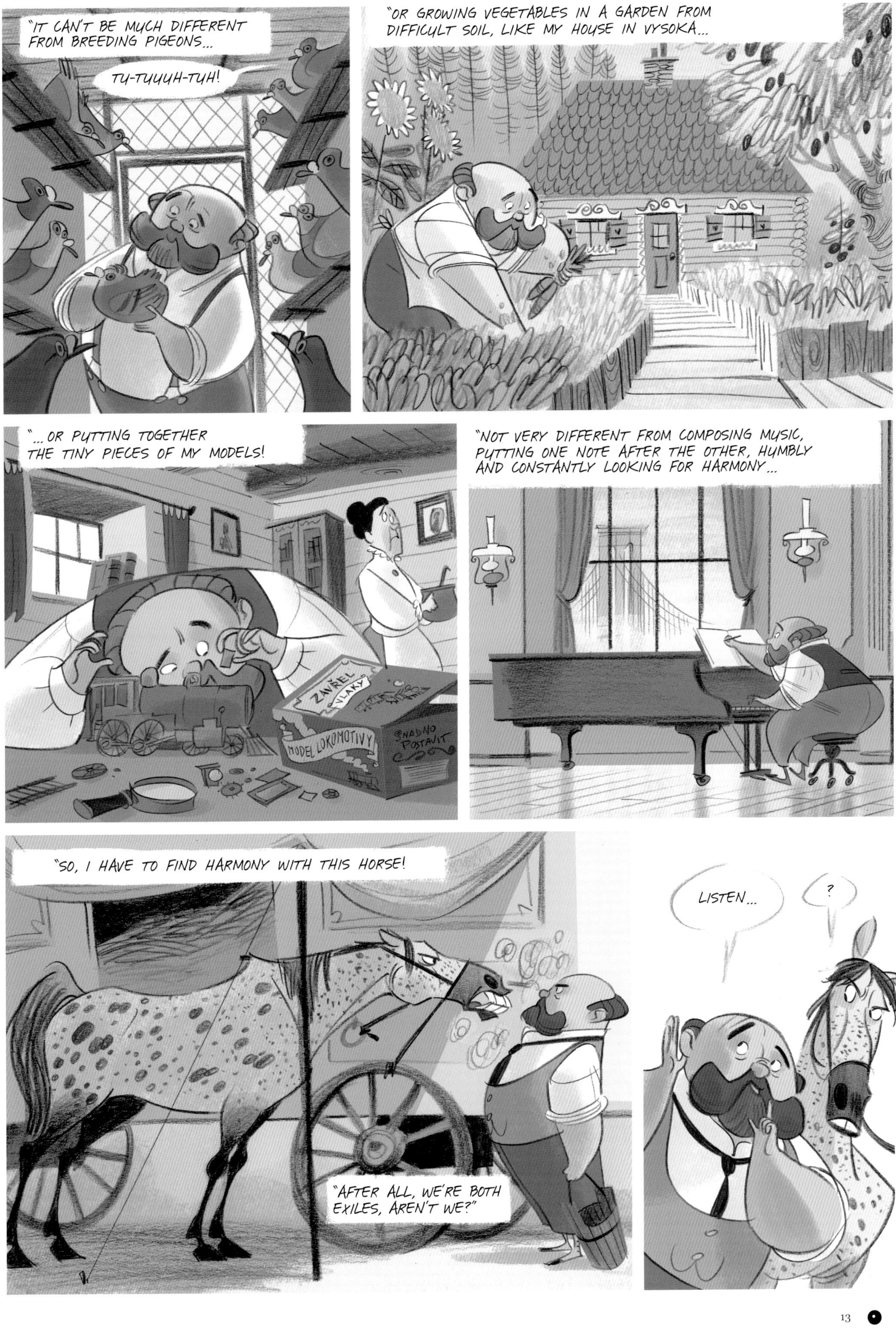
"IT CAN'T BE MUCH DIFFERENT FROM BREEDING PIGEONS...
TU-TUUUH-TUH!
"OR GROWING VEGETABLES IN A GARDEN FROM DIFFICULT SOIL, LIKE MY HOUSE IN VYSOKA...
"... OR PUTTING TOGETHER THE TINY PIECES OF MY MODELS!
ZAVŘEL
VLAKY
MODEL LOKOMOTIVY
SNADNO POSTAVIT
"NOT VERY DIFFERENT FROM COMPOSING MUSIC, PUTTING ONE NOTE AFTER THE OTHER, HUMBLY AND CONSTANTLY LOOKING FOR HARMONY...
"SO, I HAVE TO FIND HARMONY WITH THIS HORSE!
"AFTER ALL, WE'RE BOTH EXILES, AREN'T WE?"
LISTEN...
?

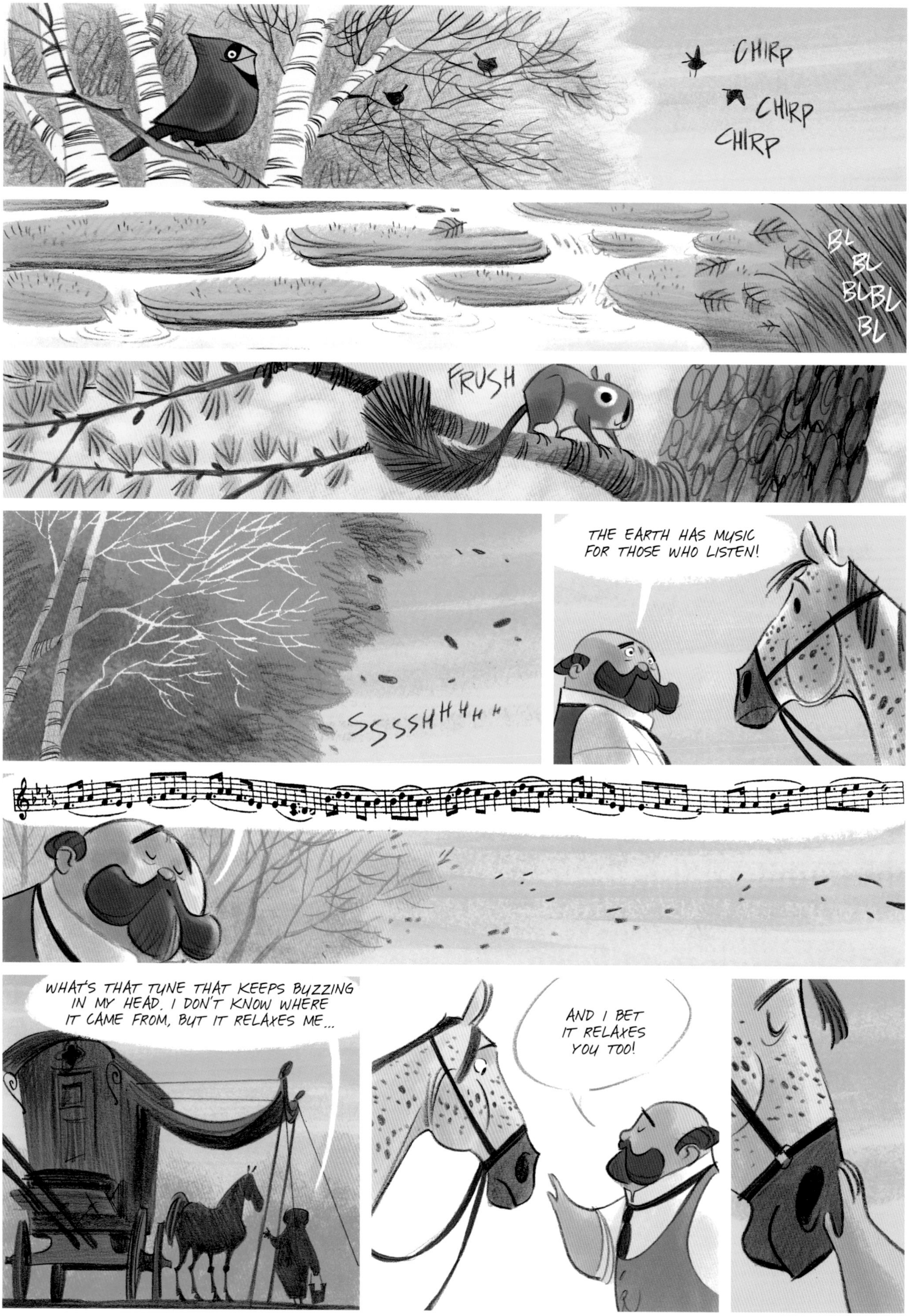
CHIRP
CHIRP
CHIRP
BL
BL
BLBL
BL
FRUSH
SSSSHHHHH
THE EARTH HAS MUSIC FOR THOSE WHO LISTEN!
WHAT'S THAT TUNE THAT KEEPS BUZZING IN MY HEAD. I DON'T KNOW WHERE IT CAME FROM, BUT IT RELAXES ME...
AND I BET IT RELAXES YOU TOO!

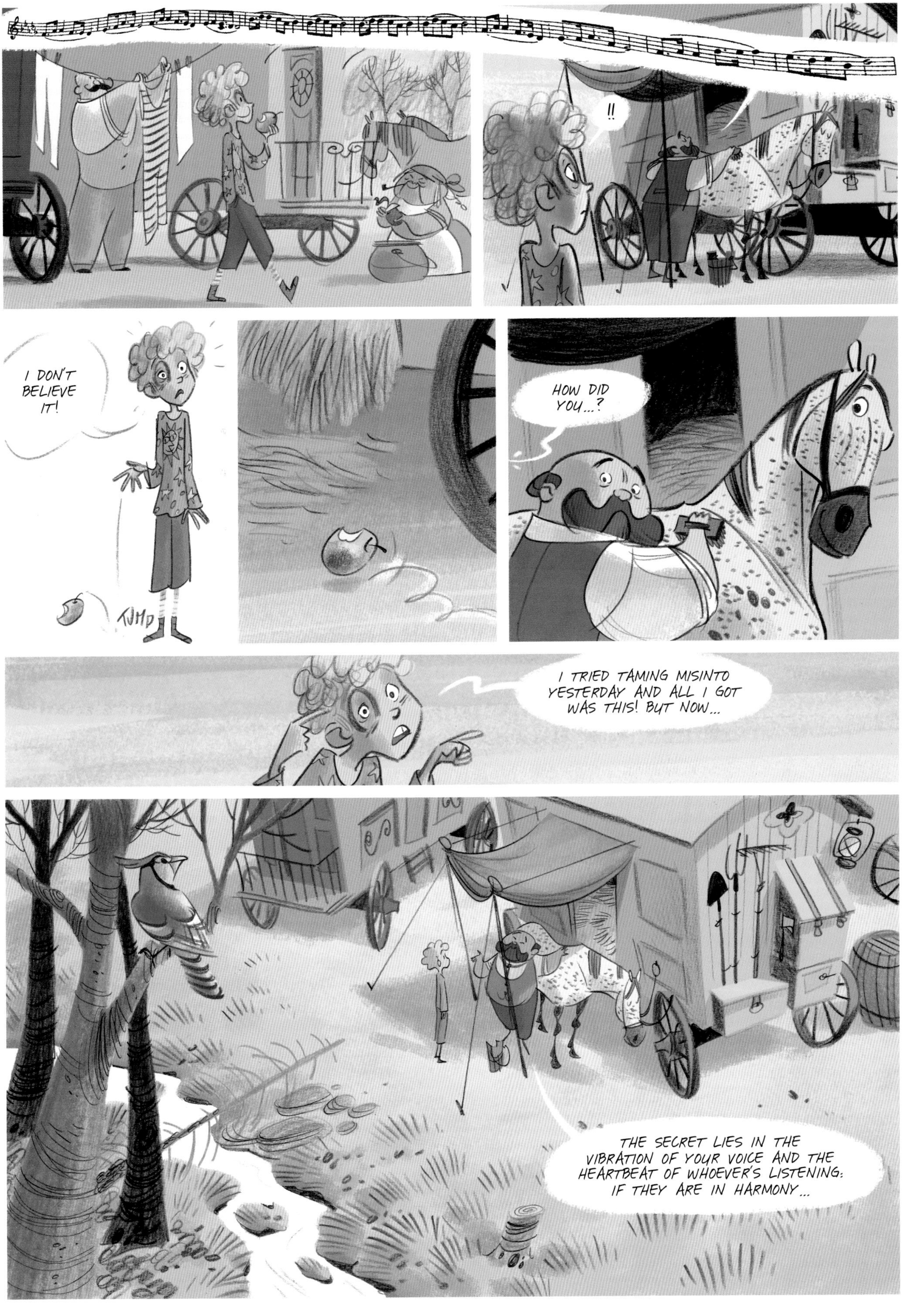
!!
I DON'T BELIEVE IT!
THUMP
HOW DID YOU...?
I TRIED TAMING MISINTO YESTERDAY AND ALL I GOT WAS THIS! BUT NOW...
THE SECRET LIES IN THE VIBRATION OF YOUR VOICE AND THE HEARTBEAT OF WHOEVER'S LISTENING: IF THEY ARE IN HARMONY...

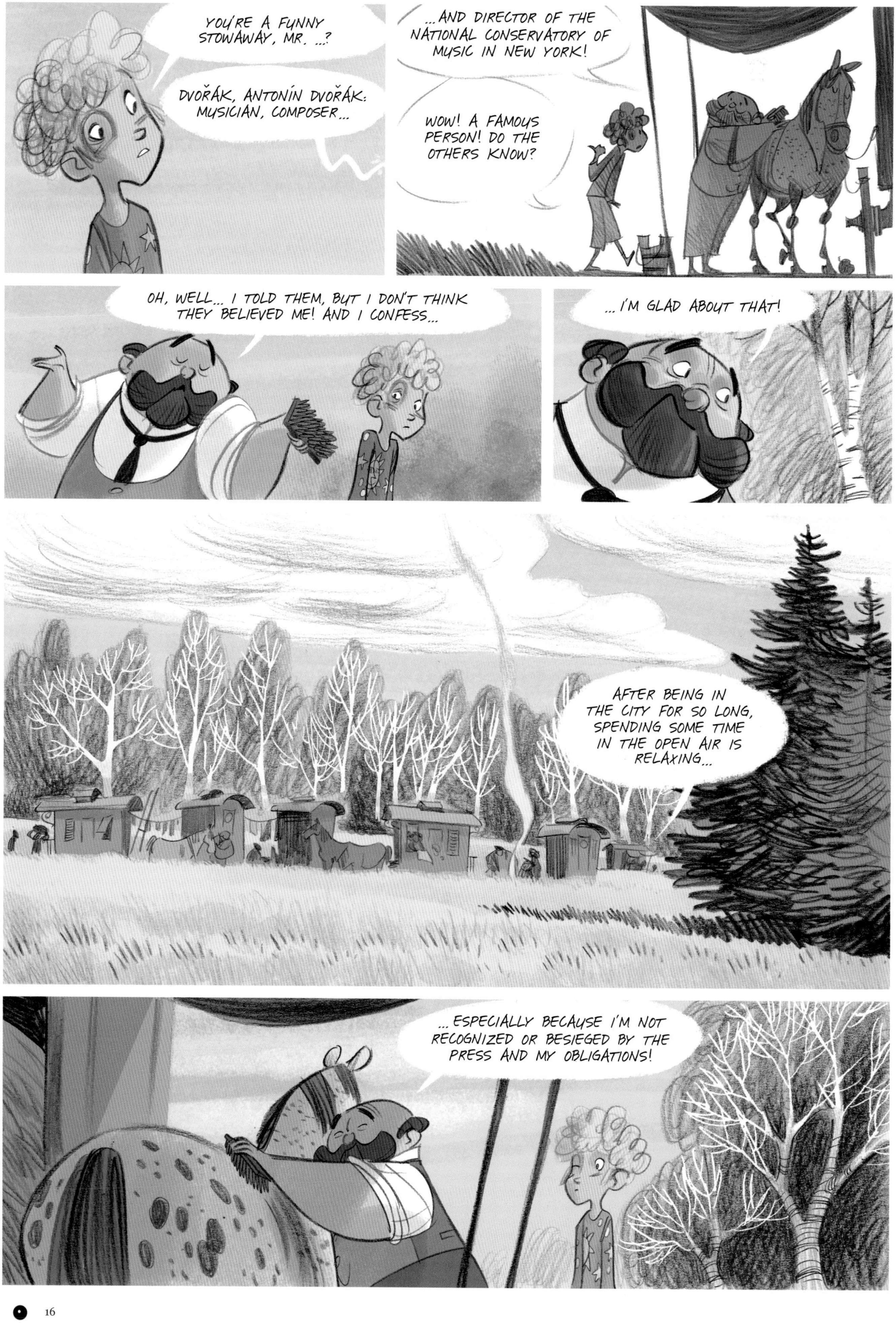
YOU'RE A FUNNY STOWAWAY, MR. ...?
DVOŘÁK, ANTONÍN DVOŘÁK: MUSICIAN, COMPOSER...
...AND DIRECTOR OF THE NATIONAL CONSERVATORY OF MUSIC IN NEW YORK!
WOW! A FAMOUS PERSON! DO THE OTHERS KNOW?
OH, WELL... I TOLD THEM, BUT I DON'T THINK THEY BELIEVED ME! AND I CONFESS...
...I'M GLAD ABOUT THAT!
AFTER BEING IN THE CITY FOR SO LONG, SPENDING SOME TIME IN THE OPEN AIR IS RELAXING...
...ESPECIALLY BECAUSE I'M NOT RECOGNIZED OR BESIEGED BY THE PRESS AND MY OBLIGATIONS!

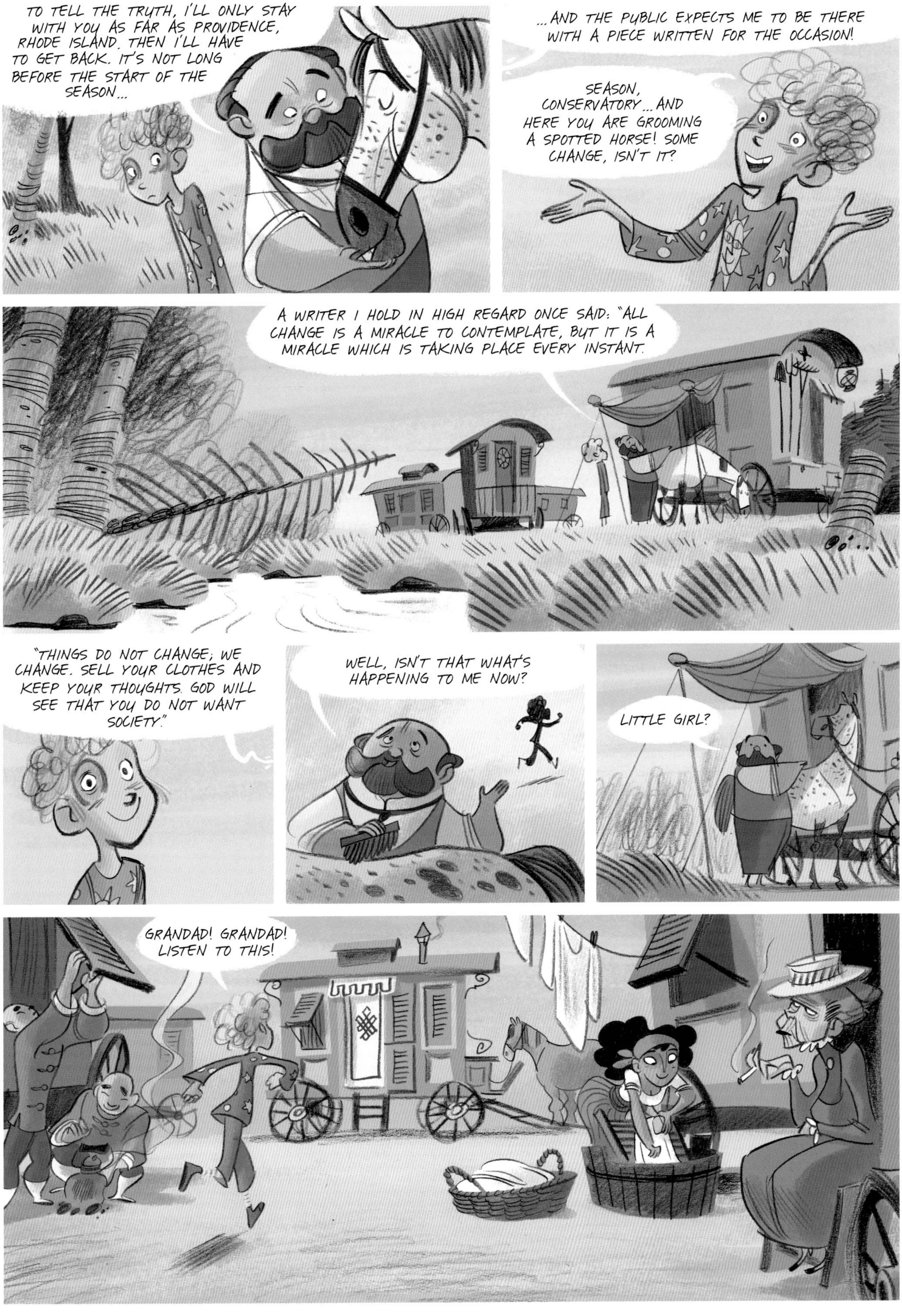
TO TELL THE TRUTH, I'LL ONLY STAY WITH YOU AS FAR AS PROVIDENCE, RHODE ISLAND. THEN I'LL HAVE TO GET BACK. IT'S NOT LONG BEFORE THE START OF THE SEASON...
...AND THE PUBLIC EXPECTS ME TO BE THERE WITH A PIECE WRITTEN FOR THE OCCASION!
SEASON, CONSERVATORY... AND HERE YOU ARE GROOMING A SPOTTED HORSE! SOME CHANGE, ISN'T IT?
A WRITER I HOLD IN HIGH REGARD ONCE SAID: "ALL CHANGE IS A MIRACLE TO CONTEMPLATE, BUT IT IS A MIRACLE WHICH IS TAKING PLACE EVERY INSTANT.
"THINGS DO NOT CHANGE; WE CHANGE. SELL YOUR CLOTHES AND KEEP YOUR THOUGHTS. GOD WILL SEE THAT YOU DO NOT WANT SOCIETY."
WELL, ISN'T THAT WHAT'S HAPPENING TO ME NOW?
LITTLE GIRL?
GRANDAD! GRANDAD! LISTEN TO THIS!

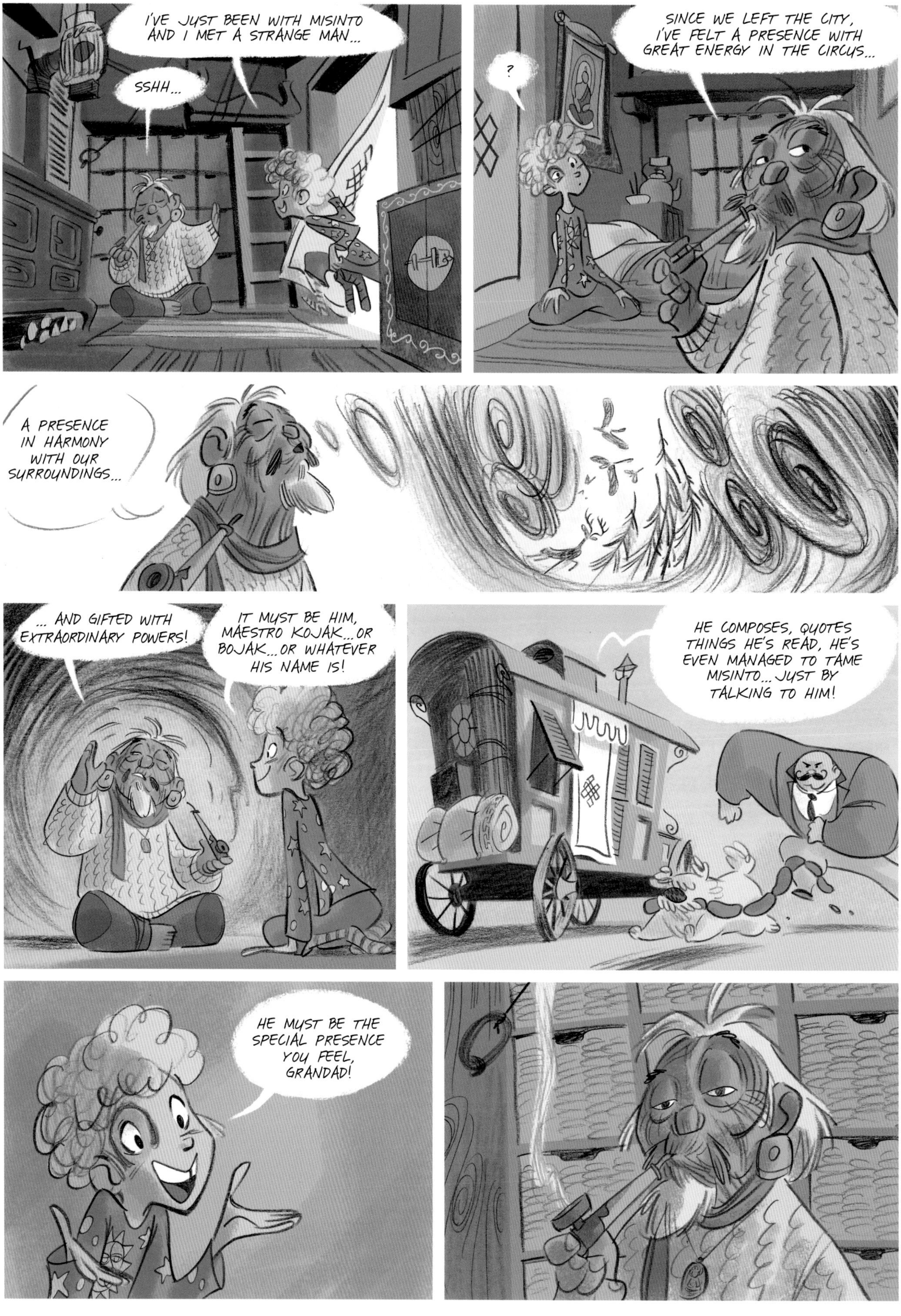
I'VE JUST BEEN WITH MISINTO AND I MET A STRANGE MAN...
SSHH...
?
SINCE WE LEFT THE CITY, I'VE FELT A PRESENCE WITH GREAT ENERGY IN THE CIRCUS...
A PRESENCE IN HARMONY WITH OUR SURROUNDINGS...
... AND GIFTED WITH EXTRAORDINARY POWERS!
IT MUST BE HIM, MAESTRO KOJAK... OR BOJAK... OR WHATEVER HIS NAME IS!
HE COMPOSES, QUOTES THINGS HE'S READ, HE'S EVEN MANAGED TO TAME MISINTO... JUST BY TALKING TO HIM!
HE MUST BE THE SPECIAL PRESENCE YOU FEEL, GRANDAD!

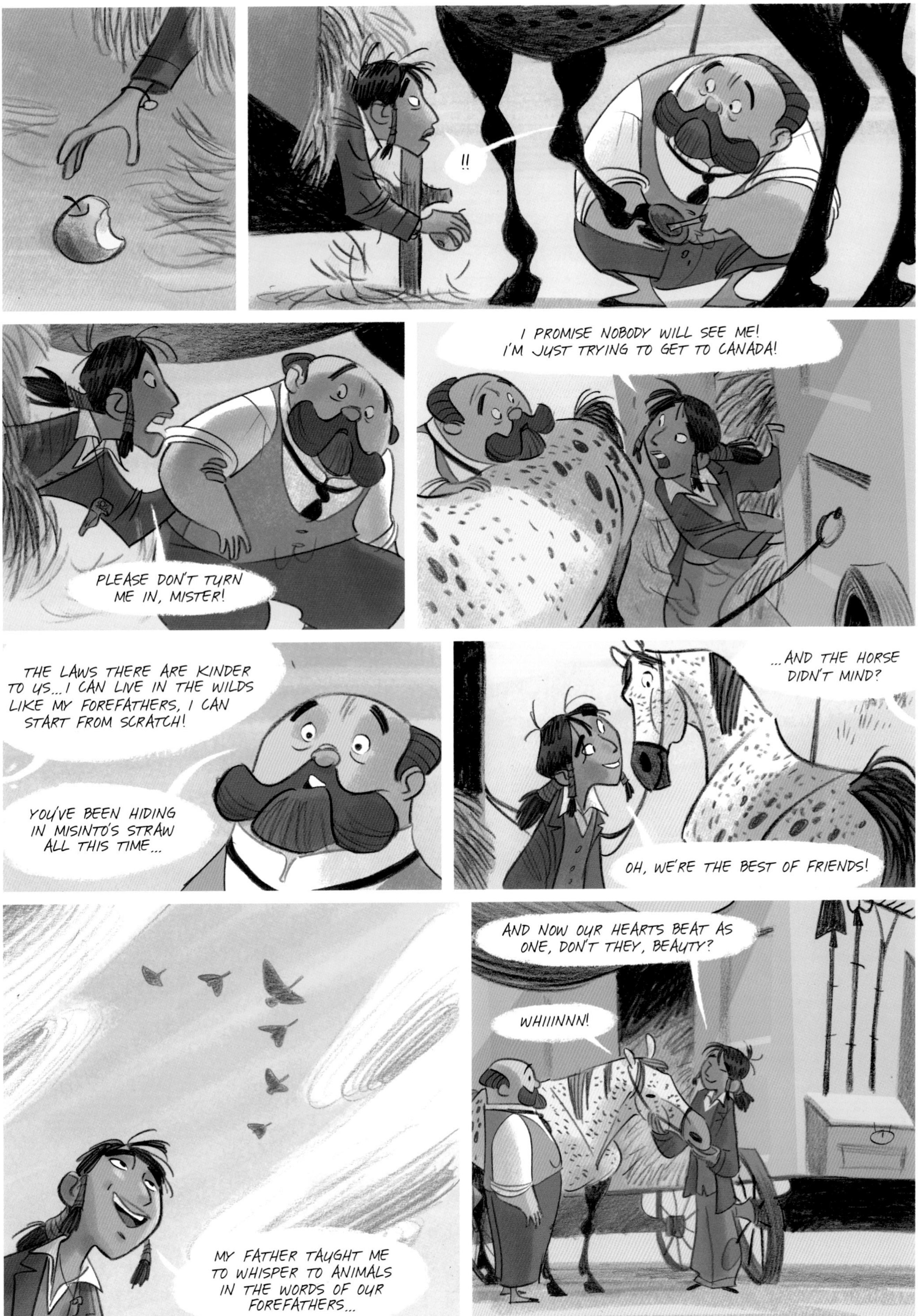
!!
PLEASE DON'T TURN ME IN, MISTER!
I PROMISE NOBODY WILL SEE ME! I'M JUST TRYING TO GET TO CANADA!
THE LAWS THERE ARE KINDER TO US... I CAN LIVE IN THE WILDS LIKE MY FOREFATHERS, I CAN START FROM SCRATCH!
YOU'VE BEEN HIDING IN MISINTO'S STRAW ALL THIS TIME...
...AND THE HORSE DIDN'T MIND?
OH, WE'RE THE BEST OF FRIENDS!
MY FATHER TAUGHT ME TO WHISPER TO ANIMALS IN THE WORDS OF OUR FOREFATHERS...
AND NOW OUR HEARTS BEAT AS ONE, DON'T THEY, BEAUTY?
WHIIINNN!

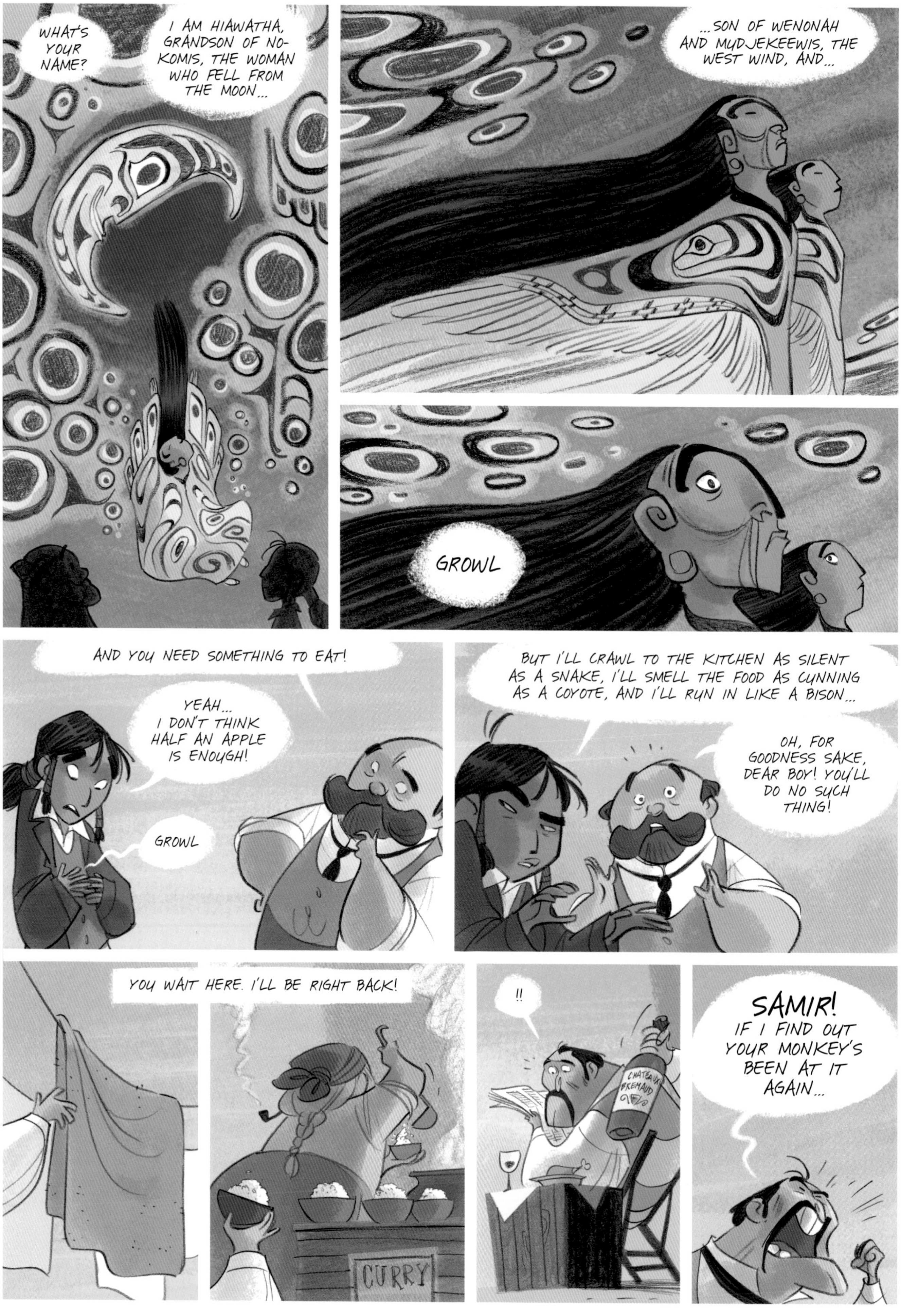
WHAT'S YOUR NAME?
I AM HIAWATHA, GRANDSON OF NO-KOMIS, THE WOMAN WHO FELL FROM THE MOON...
...SON OF WENONAH AND MUDJEKEEWIS, THE WEST WIND, AND...
GROWL
AND YOU NEED SOMETHING TO EAT!
YEAH... I DON'T THINK HALF AN APPLE IS ENOUGH!
GROWL
BUT I'LL CRAWL TO THE KITCHEN AS SILENT AS A SNAKE, I'LL SMELL THE FOOD AS CUNNING AS A COYOTE, AND I'LL RUN IN LIKE A BISON...
OH, FOR GOODNESS SAKE, DEAR BOY! YOU'LL DO NO SUCH THING!
YOU WAIT HERE. I'LL BE RIGHT BACK!
CURRY
!!
CHATEAU FREMAUD
SAMIR!
IF I FIND OUT YOUR MONKEY'S BEEN AT IT AGAIN...

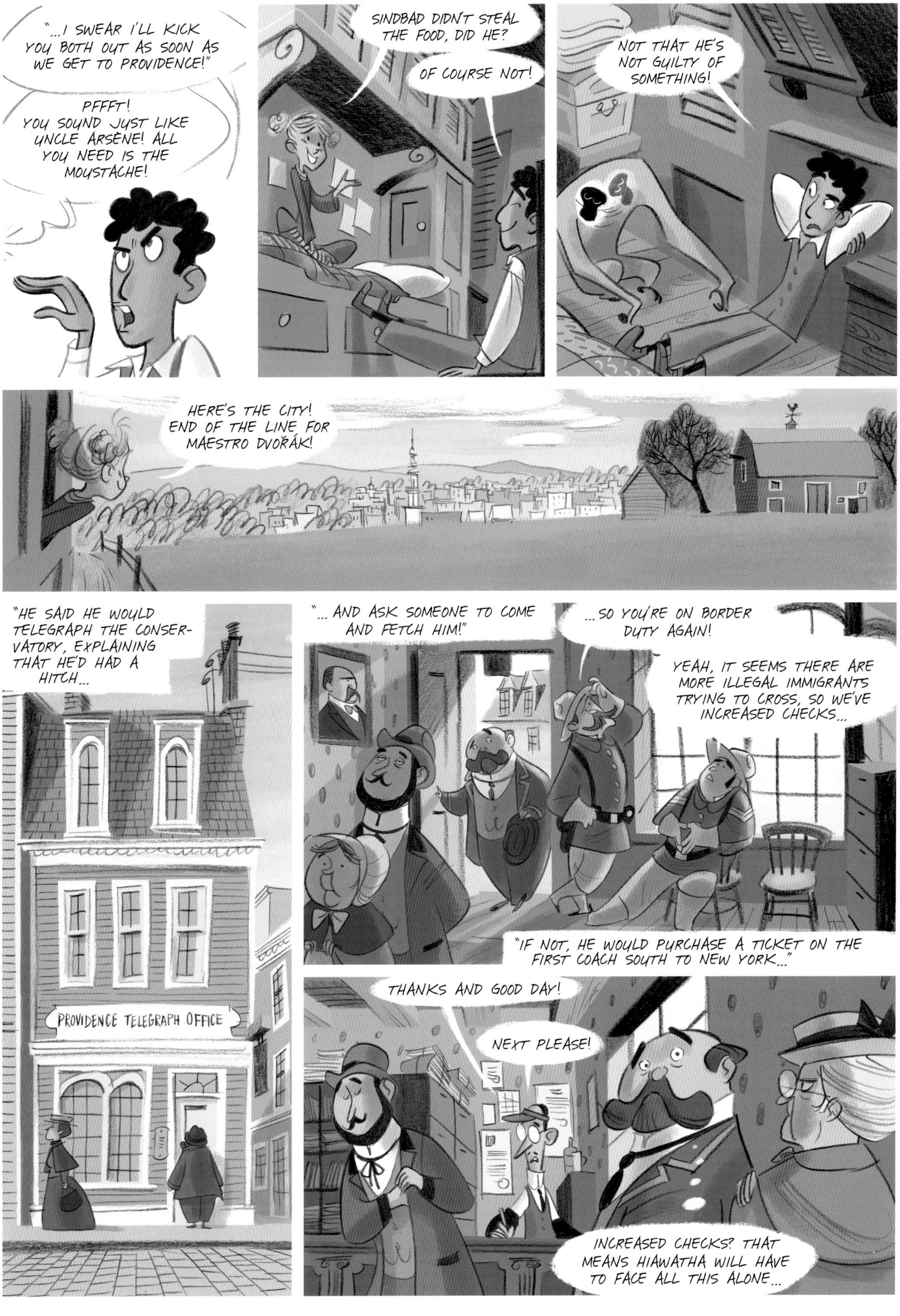
"...I SWEAR I'LL KICK YOU BOTH OUT AS SOON AS WE GET TO PROVIDENCE!"
PFFFT! YOU SOUND JUST LIKE UNCLE ARSÈNE! ALL YOU NEED IS THE MOUSTACHE!
SINDBAD DIDN'T STEAL THE FOOD, DID HE?
OF COURSE NOT!
NOT THAT HE'S NOT GUILTY OF SOMETHING!
HERE'S THE CITY! END OF THE LINE FOR MAESTRO DVOŘÁK!
"HE SAID HE WOULD TELEGRAPH THE CONSER-VATORY, EXPLAINING THAT HE'D HAD A HITCH...
PROVIDENCE TELEGRAPH OFFICE
"... AND ASK SOMEONE TO COME AND FETCH HIM!"
...SO YOU'RE ON BORDER DUTY AGAIN!
YEAH, IT SEEMS THERE ARE MORE ILLEGAL IMMIGRANTS TRYING TO CROSS, SO WE'VE INCREASED CHECKS...
"IF NOT, HE WOULD PURCHASE A TICKET ON THE FIRST COACH SOUTH TO NEW YORK..."
THANKS AND GOOD DAY!
NEXT PLEASE!
INCREASED CHECKS? THAT MEANS HIAWATHA WILL HAVE TO FACE ALL THIS ALONE...

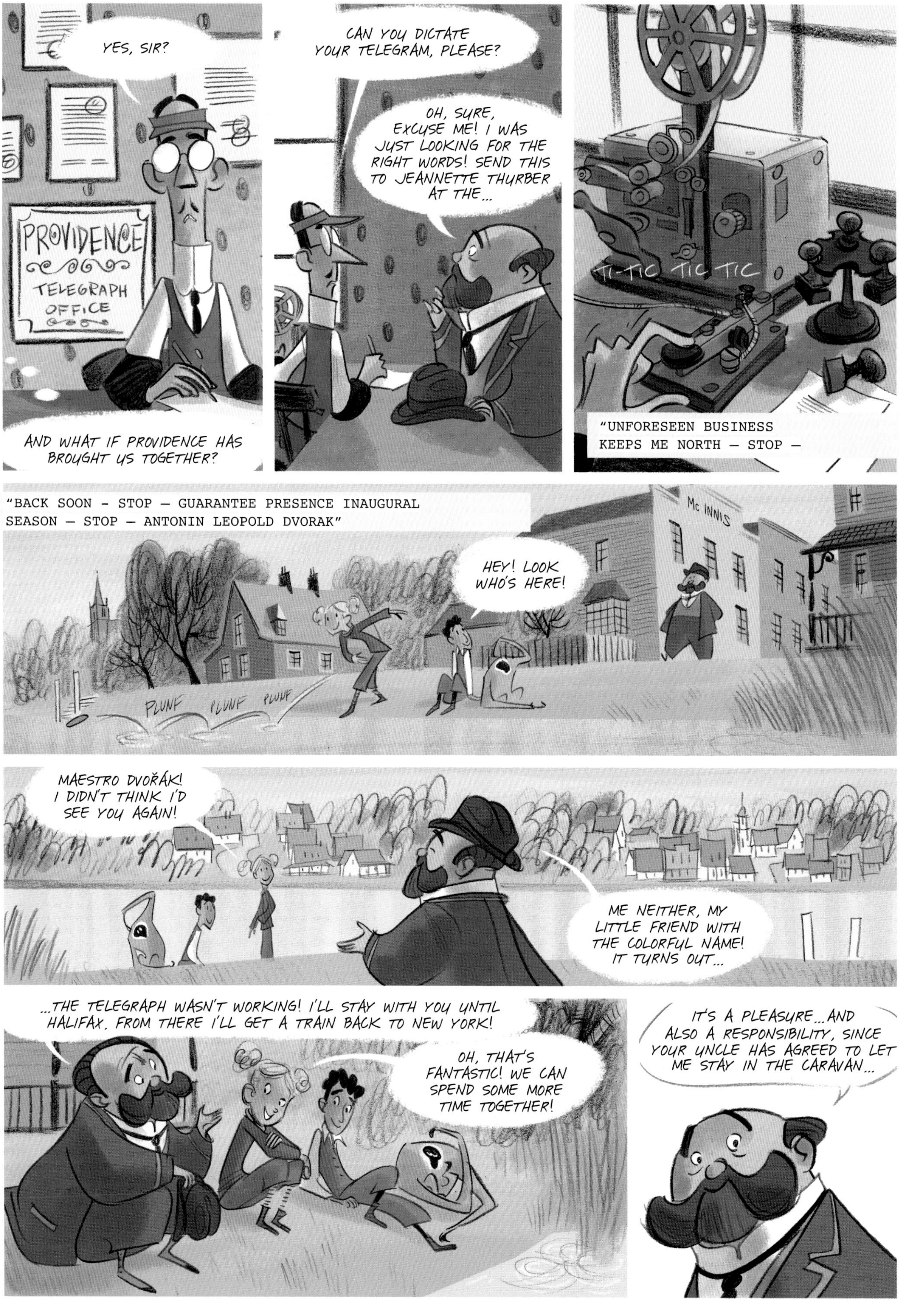
YES, SIR?
AND WHAT IF PROVIDENCE HAS BROUGHT US TOGETHER?
PROVIDENCE TELEGRAPH OFFICE
CAN YOU DICTATE YOUR TELEGRAM, PLEASE?
OH, SURE, EXCUSE ME! I WAS JUST LOOKING FOR THE RIGHT WORDS! SEND THIS TO JEANNETTE THURBER AT THE...
TI-TIC TIC TIC
"UNFORESEEN BUSINESS KEEPS ME NORTH – STOP –
"BACK SOON - STOP – GUARANTEE PRESENCE INAUGURAL SEASON – STOP – ANTONIN LEOPOLD DVORAK"
Mc INNIS
HEY! LOOK WHO'S HERE!
PLUNF PLUNF PLUNF
MAESTRO DVOŘÁK! I DIDN'T THINK I'D SEE YOU AGAIN!
ME NEITHER, MY LITTLE FRIEND WITH THE COLORFUL NAME! IT TURNS OUT...
...THE TELEGRAPH WASN'T WORKING! I'LL STAY WITH YOU UNTIL HALIFAX. FROM THERE I'LL GET A TRAIN BACK TO NEW YORK!
OH, THAT'S FANTASTIC! WE CAN SPEND SOME MORE TIME TOGETHER!
IT'S A PLEASURE... AND ALSO A RESPONSIBILITY, SINCE YOUR UNCLE HAS AGREED TO LET ME STAY IN THE CARAVAN...

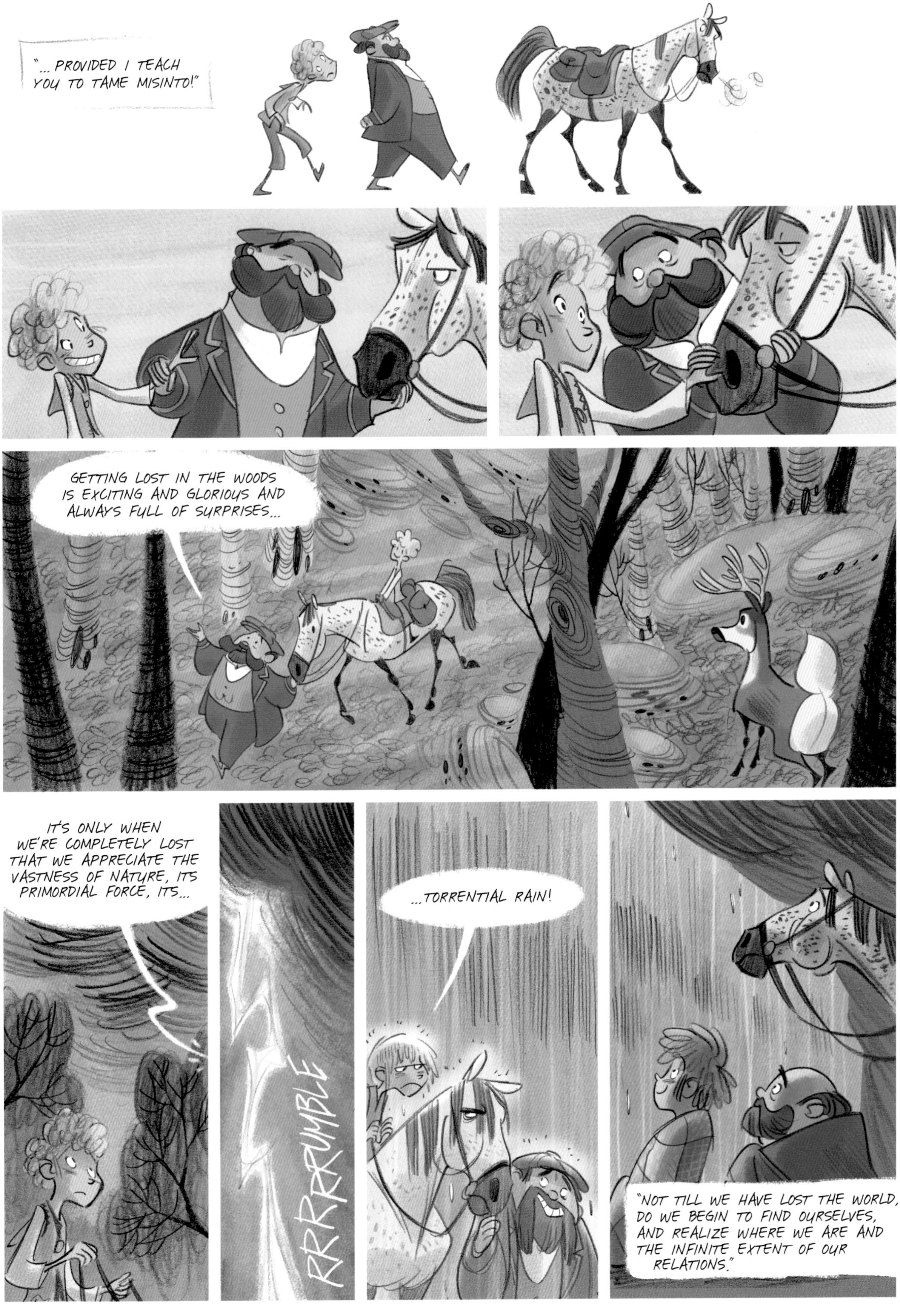
"... PROVIDED I TEACH YOU TO TAME MISINTO!"
GETTING LOST IN THE WOODS IS EXCITING AND GLORIOUS AND ALWAYS FULL OF SURPRISES...
IT'S ONLY WHEN WE'RE COMPLETELY LOST THAT WE APPRECIATE THE VASTNESS OF NATURE, ITS PRIMORDIAL FORCE, ITS...
RRRRRRUMBLE
...TORRENTIAL RAIN!
"NOT TILL WE HAVE LOST THE WORLD, DO WE BEGIN TO FIND OURSELVES, AND REALIZE WHERE WE ARE AND THE INFINITE EXTENT OF OUR RELATIONS."

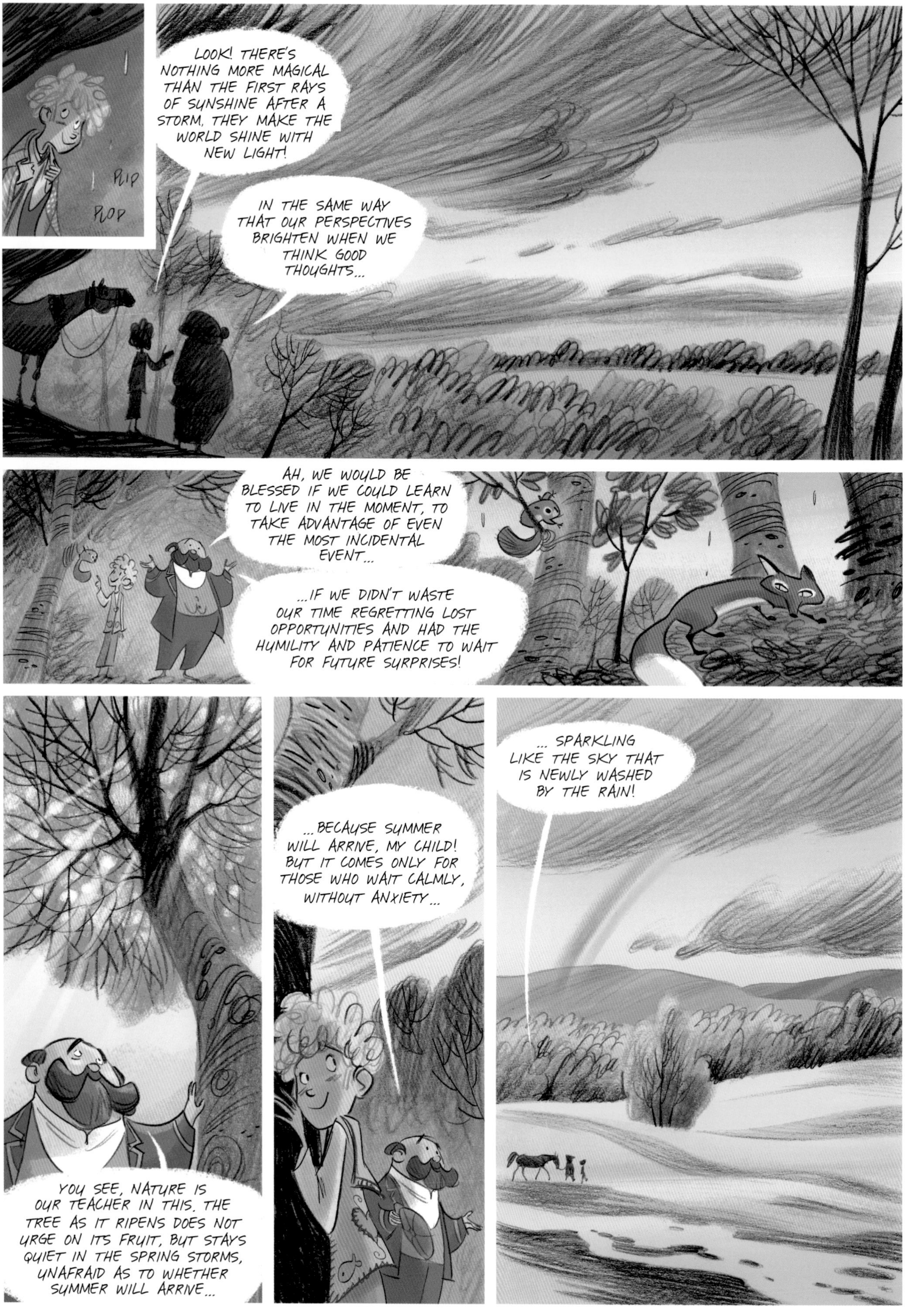
PLIP
PLOP
LOOK! THERE'S NOTHING MORE MAGICAL THAN THE FIRST RAYS OF SUNSHINE AFTER A STORM, THEY MAKE THE WORLD SHINE WITH NEW LIGHT!
IN THE SAME WAY THAT OUR PERSPECTIVES BRIGHTEN WHEN WE THINK GOOD THOUGHTS...
AH, WE WOULD BE BLESSED IF WE COULD LEARN TO LIVE IN THE MOMENT, TO TAKE ADVANTAGE OF EVEN THE MOST INCIDENTAL EVENT...
...IF WE DIDN'T WASTE OUR TIME REGRETTING LOST OPPORTUNITIES AND HAD THE HUMILITY AND PATIENCE TO WAIT FOR FUTURE SURPRISES!
YOU SEE, NATURE IS OUR TEACHER IN THIS. THE TREE AS IT RIPENS DOES NOT URGE ON ITS FRUIT, BUT STAYS QUIET IN THE SPRING STORMS, UNAFRAID AS TO WHETHER SUMMER WILL ARRIVE...
...BECAUSE SUMMER WILL ARRIVE, MY CHILD! BUT IT COMES ONLY FOR THOSE WHO WAIT CALMLY, WITHOUT ANXIETY...
... SPARKLING LIKE THE SKY THAT IS NEWLY WASHED BY THE RAIN!

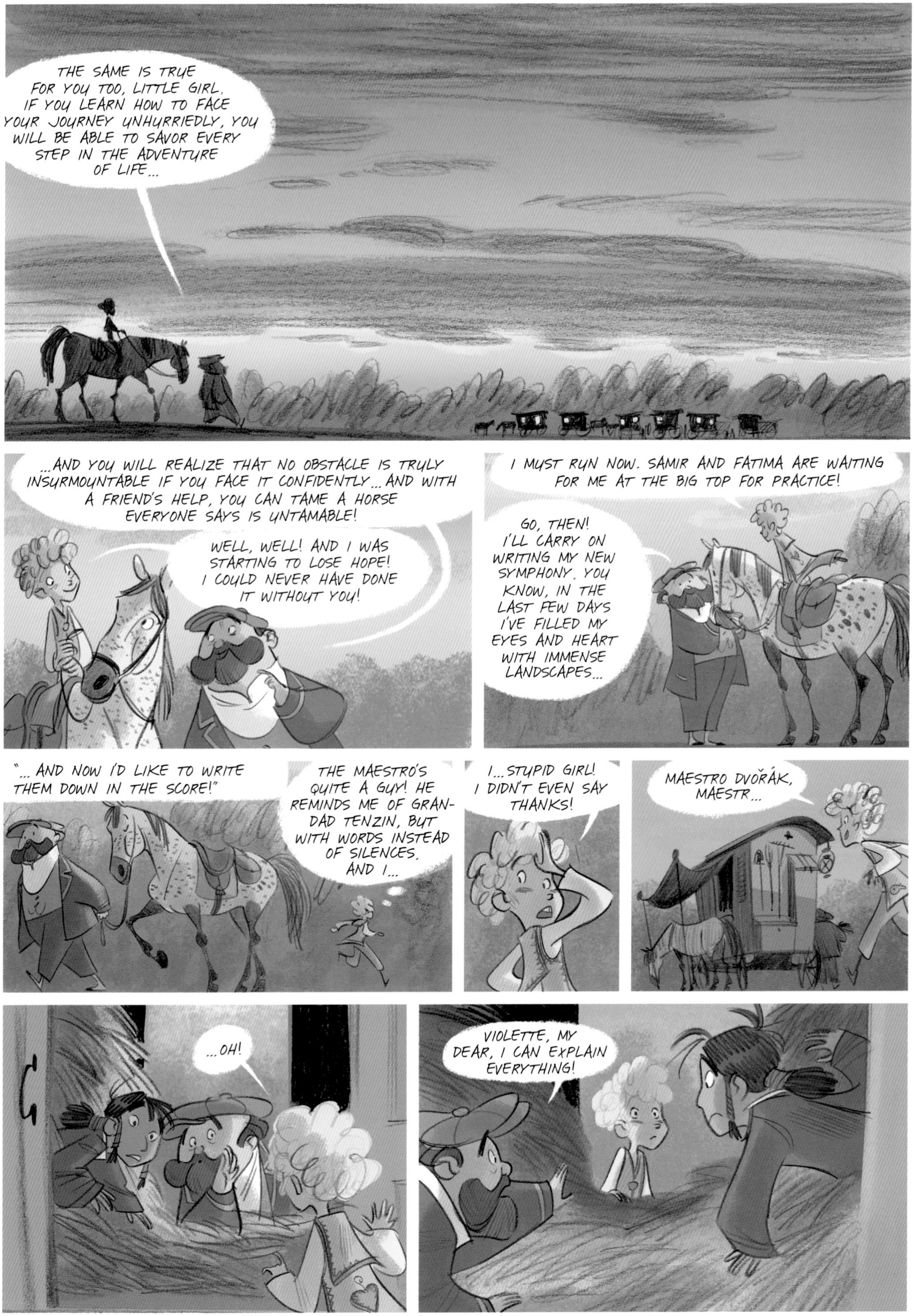
THE SAME IS TRUE FOR YOU TOO, LITTLE GIRL. IF YOU LEARN HOW TO FACE YOUR JOURNEY UNHURRIEDLY, YOU WILL BE ABLE TO SAVOR EVERY STEP IN THE ADVENTURE OF LIFE...
...AND YOU WILL REALIZE THAT NO OBSTACLE IS TRULY INSURMOUNTABLE IF YOU FACE IT CONFIDENTLY... AND WITH A FRIEND'S HELP, YOU CAN TAME A HORSE EVERYONE SAYS IS UNTAMABLE!
WELL, WELL! AND I WAS STARTING TO LOSE HOPE! I COULD NEVER HAVE DONE IT WITHOUT YOU!
I MUST RUN NOW. SAMIR AND FATIMA ARE WAITING FOR ME AT THE BIG TOP FOR PRACTICE!
GO, THEN! I'LL CARRY ON WRITING MY NEW SYMPHONY. YOU KNOW, IN THE LAST FEW DAYS I'VE FILLED MY EYES AND HEART WITH IMMENSE LANDSCAPES...
"... AND NOW I'D LIKE TO WRITE THEM DOWN IN THE SCORE!"
THE MAESTRO'S QUITE A GUY! HE REMINDS ME OF GRAN-DAD TENZIN, BUT WITH WORDS INSTEAD OF SILENCES. AND I...
I... STUPID GIRL! I DIDN'T EVEN SAY THANKS!
MAESTRO DVOŘÁK, MAESTR...
...OH!
VIOLETTE, MY DEAR, I CAN EXPLAIN EVERYTHING!

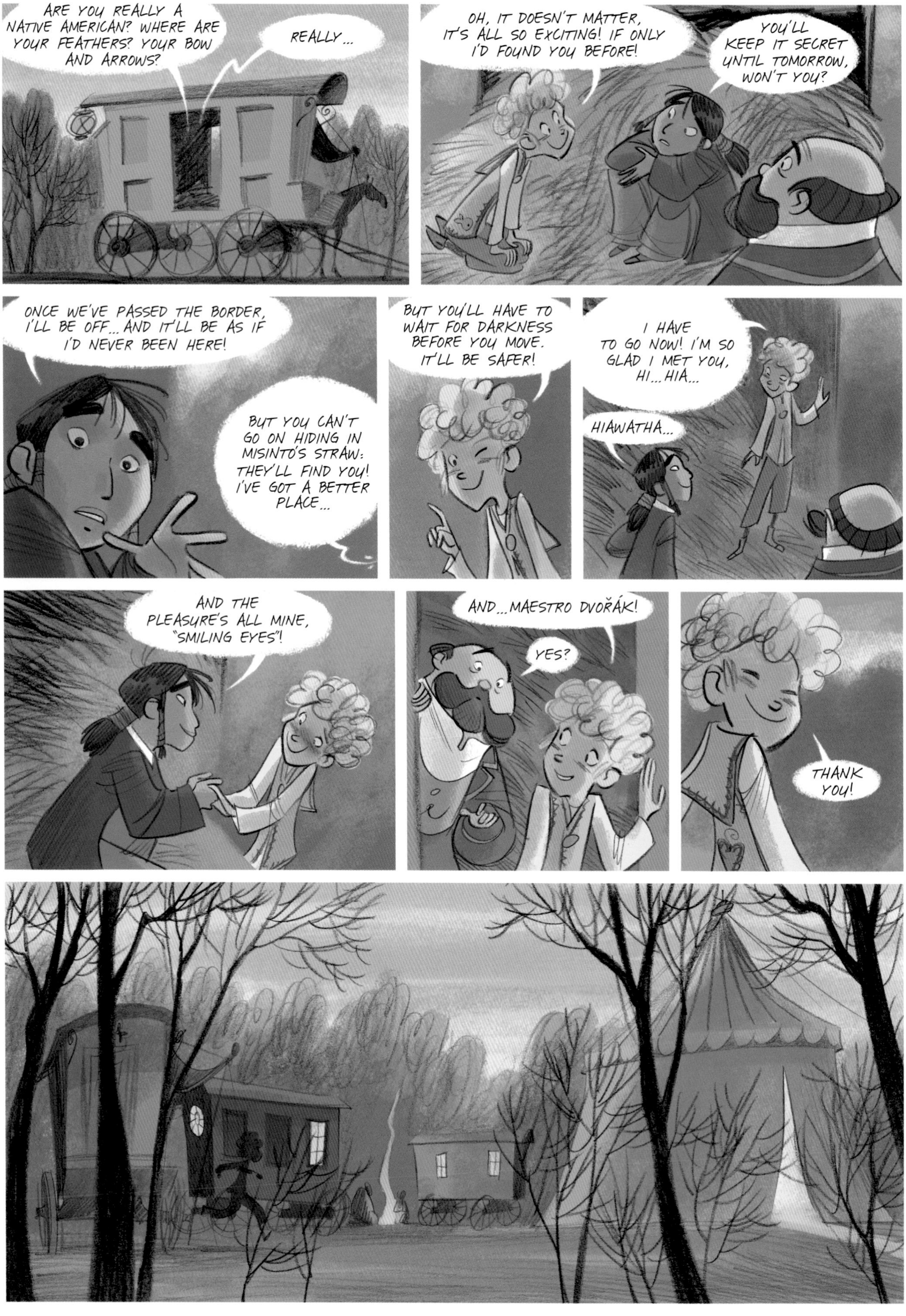
ARE YOU REALLY A NATIVE AMERICAN? WHERE ARE YOUR FEATHERS? YOUR BOW AND ARROWS?
REALLY...
OH, IT DOESN'T MATTER, IT'S ALL SO EXCITING! IF ONLY I'D FOUND YOU BEFORE!
YOU'LL KEEP IT SECRET UNTIL TOMORROW, WON'T YOU?
ONCE WE'VE PASSED THE BORDER, I'LL BE OFF... AND IT'LL BE AS IF I'D NEVER BEEN HERE!
BUT YOU CAN'T GO ON HIDING IN MISINTO'S STRAW: THEY'LL FIND YOU! I'VE GOT A BETTER PLACE...
BUT YOU'LL HAVE TO WAIT FOR DARKNESS BEFORE YOU MOVE. IT'LL BE SAFER!
I HAVE TO GO NOW! I'M SO GLAD I MET YOU, HI... HIA...
HIAWATHA...
AND THE PLEASURE'S ALL MINE, "SMILING EYES"!
AND... MAESTRO DVOŘÁK!
YES?
THANK YOU!

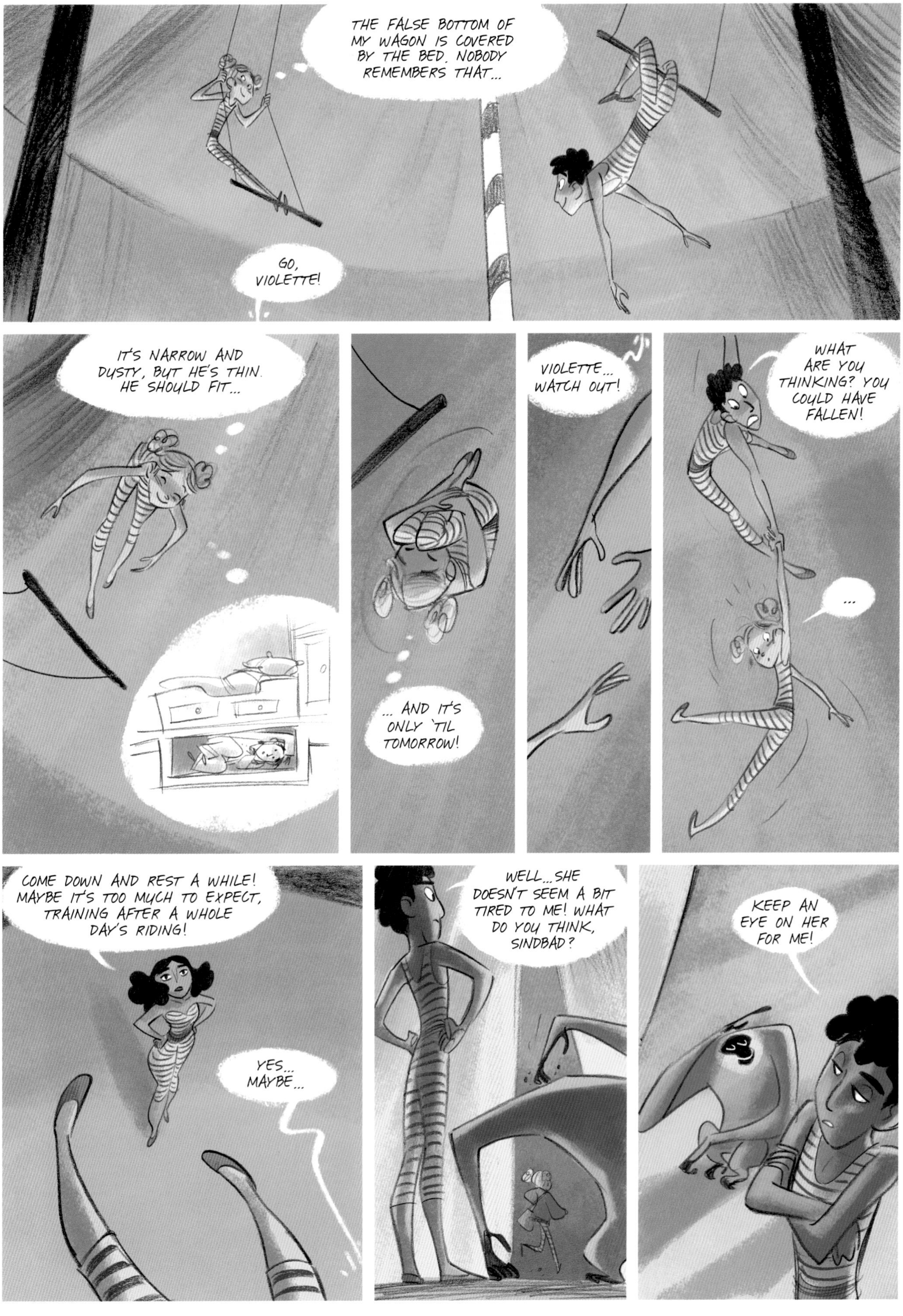
THE FALSE BOTTOM OF MY WAGON IS COVERED BY THE BED. NOBODY REMEMBERS THAT...
GO, VIOLETTE!
IT'S NARROW AND DUSTY, BUT HE'S THIN. HE SHOULD FIT...
... AND IT'S ONLY 'TIL TOMORROW!
VIOLETTE... WATCH OUT!
WHAT ARE YOU THINKING? YOU COULD HAVE FALLEN!
...
COME DOWN AND REST A WHILE! MAYBE IT'S TOO MUCH TO EXPECT, TRAINING AFTER A WHOLE DAY'S RIDING!
YES... MAYBE...
WELL... SHE DOESN'T SEEM A BIT TIRED TO ME! WHAT DO YOU THINK, SINDBAD?
KEEP AN EYE ON HER FOR ME!

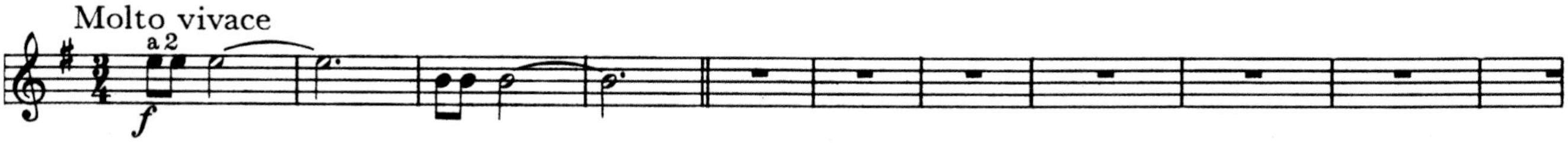
Molto vivace
a 2
f

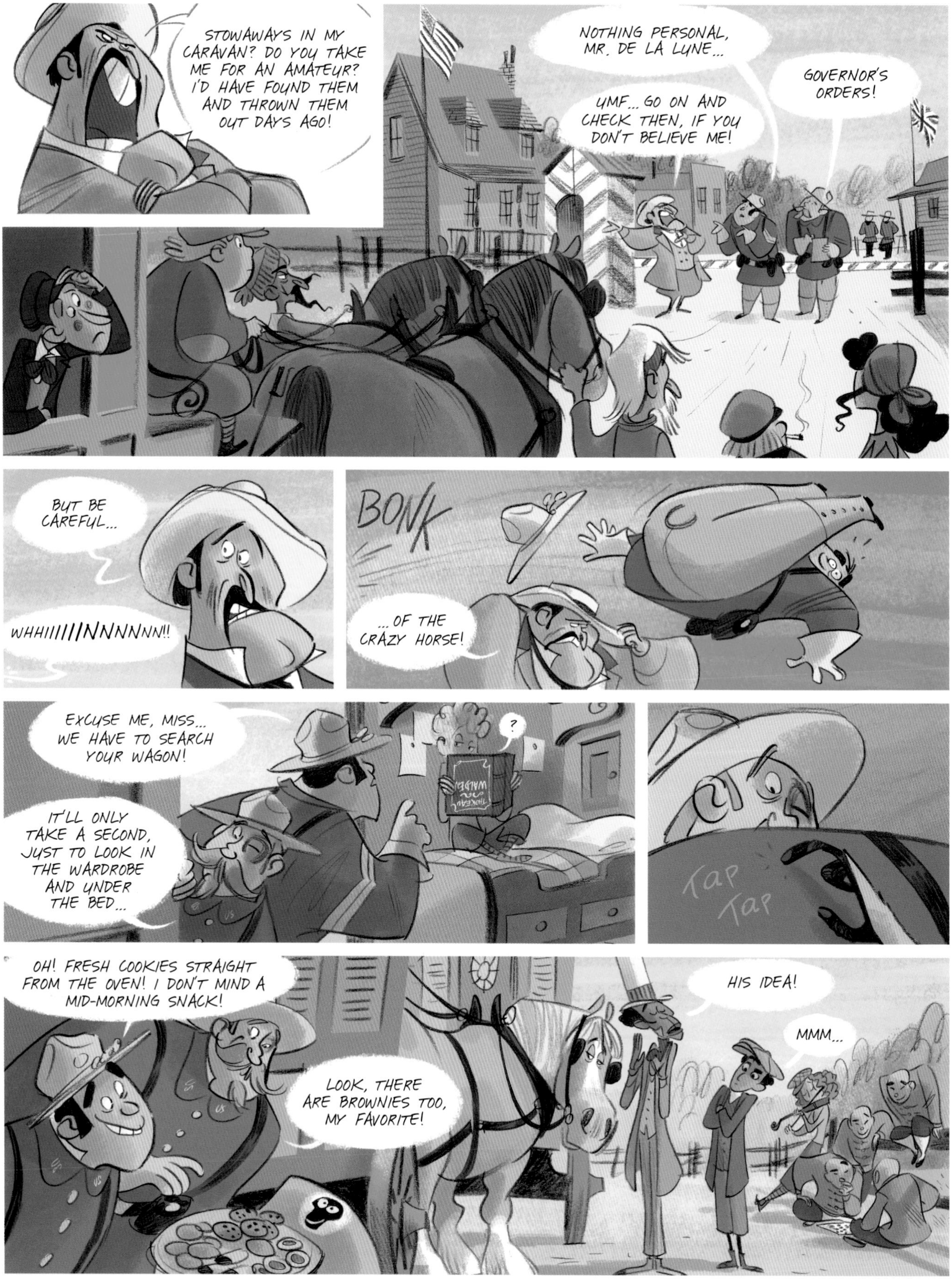
STOWAWAYS IN MY CARAVAN? DO YOU TAKE ME FOR AN AMATEUR? I'D HAVE FOUND THEM AND THROWN THEM OUT DAYS AGO!
NOTHING PERSONAL, MR. DE LA LUNE...
GOVERNOR'S ORDERS!
UMF... GO ON AND CHECK THEN, IF YOU DON'T BELIEVE ME!
BUT BE CAREFUL...
WHHIIIIIINNNNNN!!
BONK
...OF THE CRAZY HORSE!
EXCUSE ME, MISS... WE HAVE TO SEARCH YOUR WAGON!
IT'LL ONLY TAKE A SECOND, JUST TO LOOK IN THE WARDROBE AND UNDER THE BED...
?
TAP TAP
OH! FRESH COOKIES STRAIGHT FROM THE OVEN! I DON'T MIND A MID-MORNING SNACK!
LOOK, THERE ARE BROWNIES TOO, MY FAVORITE!
HIS IDEA!
MMM...

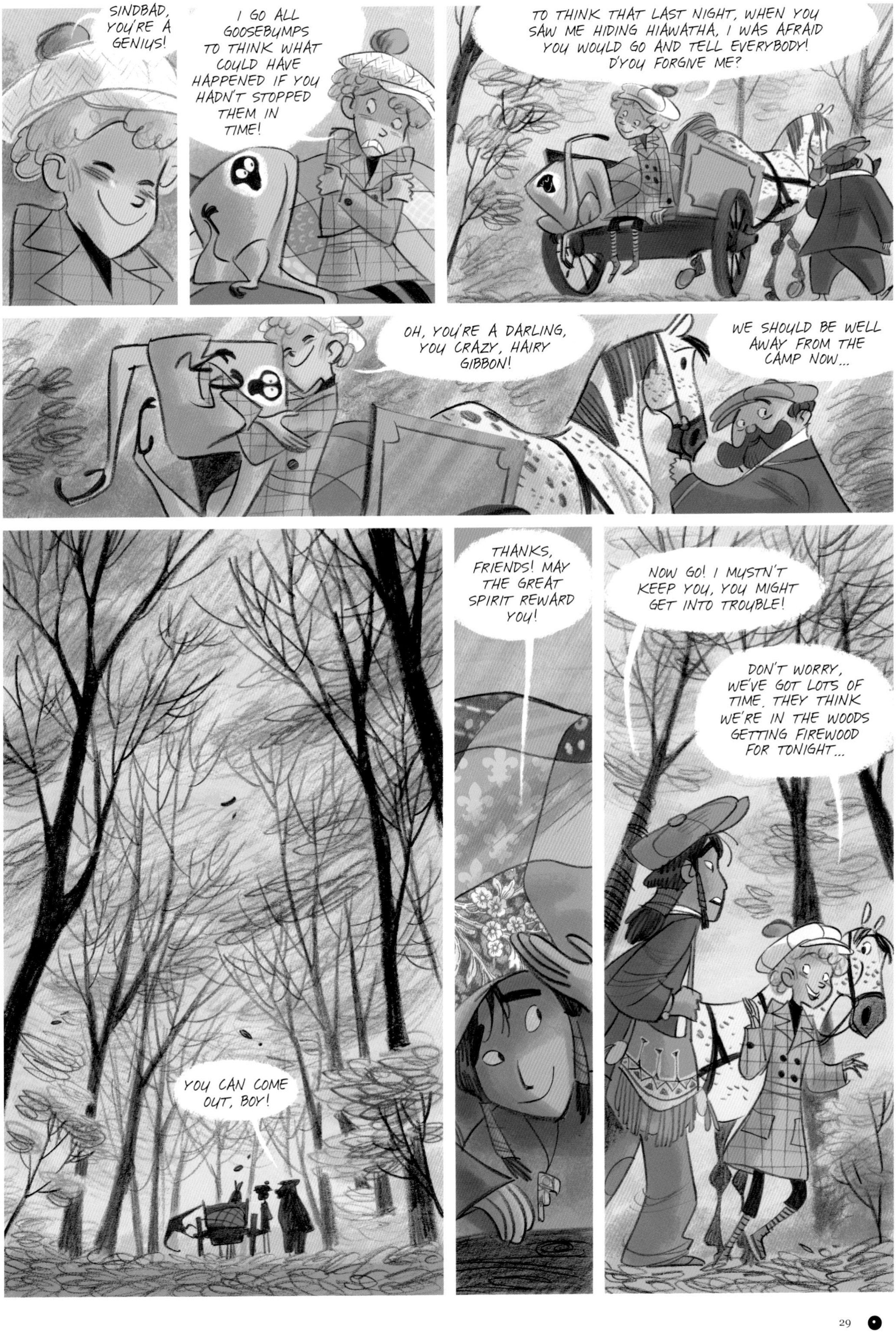
SINDBAD, YOU'RE A GENIUS!
I GO ALL GOOSEBUMPS TO THINK WHAT COULD HAVE HAPPENED IF YOU HADN'T STOPPED THEM IN TIME!
TO THINK THAT LAST NIGHT, WHEN YOU SAW ME HIDING HIAWATHA, I WAS AFRAID YOU WOULD GO AND TELL EVERYBODY! D'YOU FORGIVE ME?
OH, YOU'RE A DARLING, YOU CRAZY, HAIRY GIBBON!
WE SHOULD BE WELL AWAY FROM THE CAMP NOW...
YOU CAN COME OUT, BOY!
THANKS, FRIENDS! MAY THE GREAT SPIRIT REWARD YOU!
NOW GO! I MUSTN'T KEEP YOU, YOU MIGHT GET INTO TROUBLE!
DON'T WORRY, WE'VE GOT LOTS OF TIME. THEY THINK WE'RE IN THE WOODS GETTING FIREWOOD FOR TONIGHT...

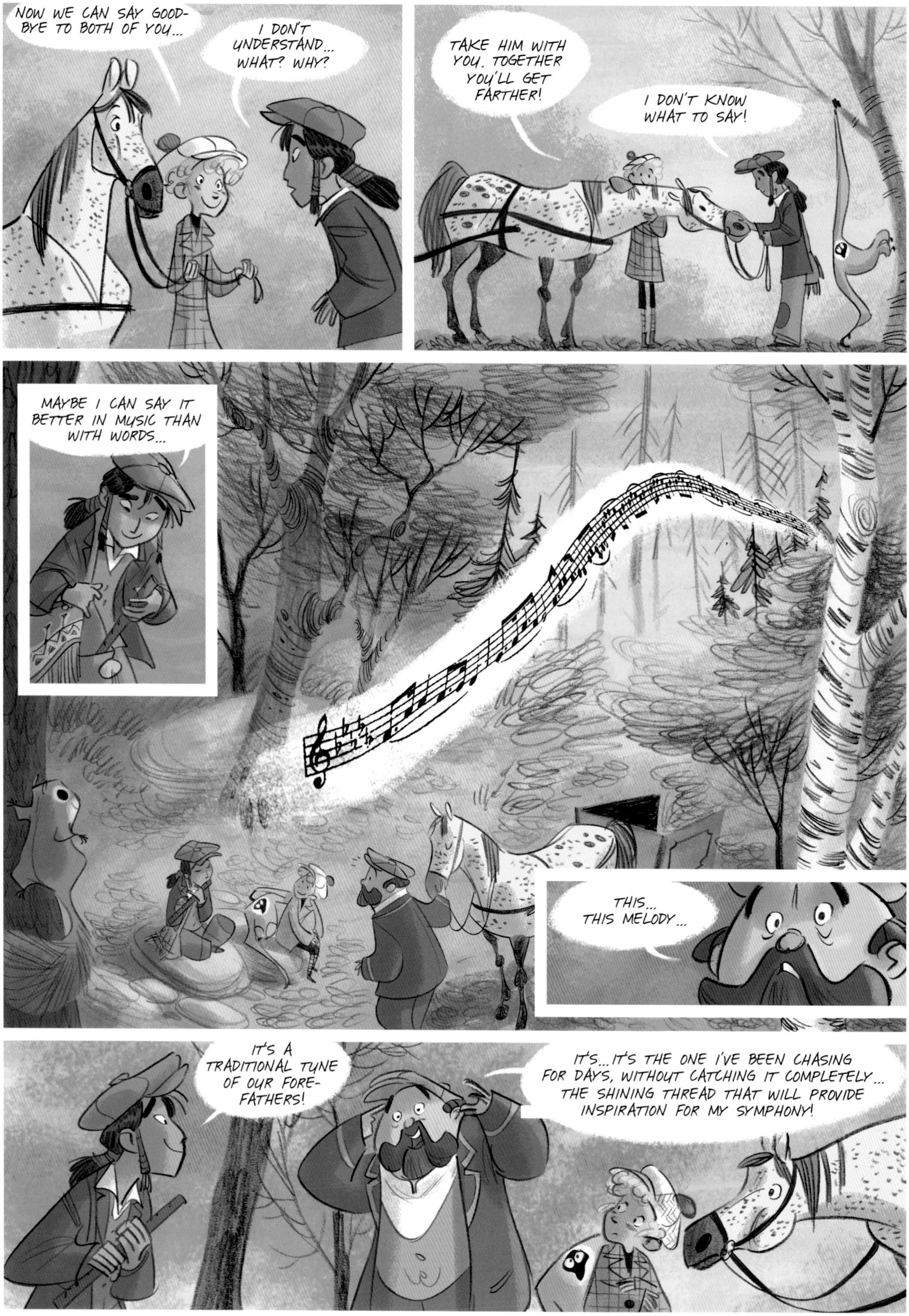
NOW WE CAN SAY GOOD-BYE TO BOTH OF YOU...
I DON'T UNDERSTAND... WHAT? WHY?
TAKE HIM WITH YOU. TOGETHER YOU'LL GET FARTHER!
I DON'T KNOW WHAT TO SAY!
MAYBE I CAN SAY IT BETTER IN MUSIC THAN WITH WORDS...
THIS... THIS MELODY...
IT'S A TRADITIONAL TUNE OF OUR FORE-FATHERS!
IT'S... IT'S THE ONE I'VE BEEN CHASING FOR DAYS, WITHOUT CATCHING IT COMPLETELY... THE SHINING THREAD THAT WILL PROVIDE INSPIRATION FOR MY SYMPHONY!

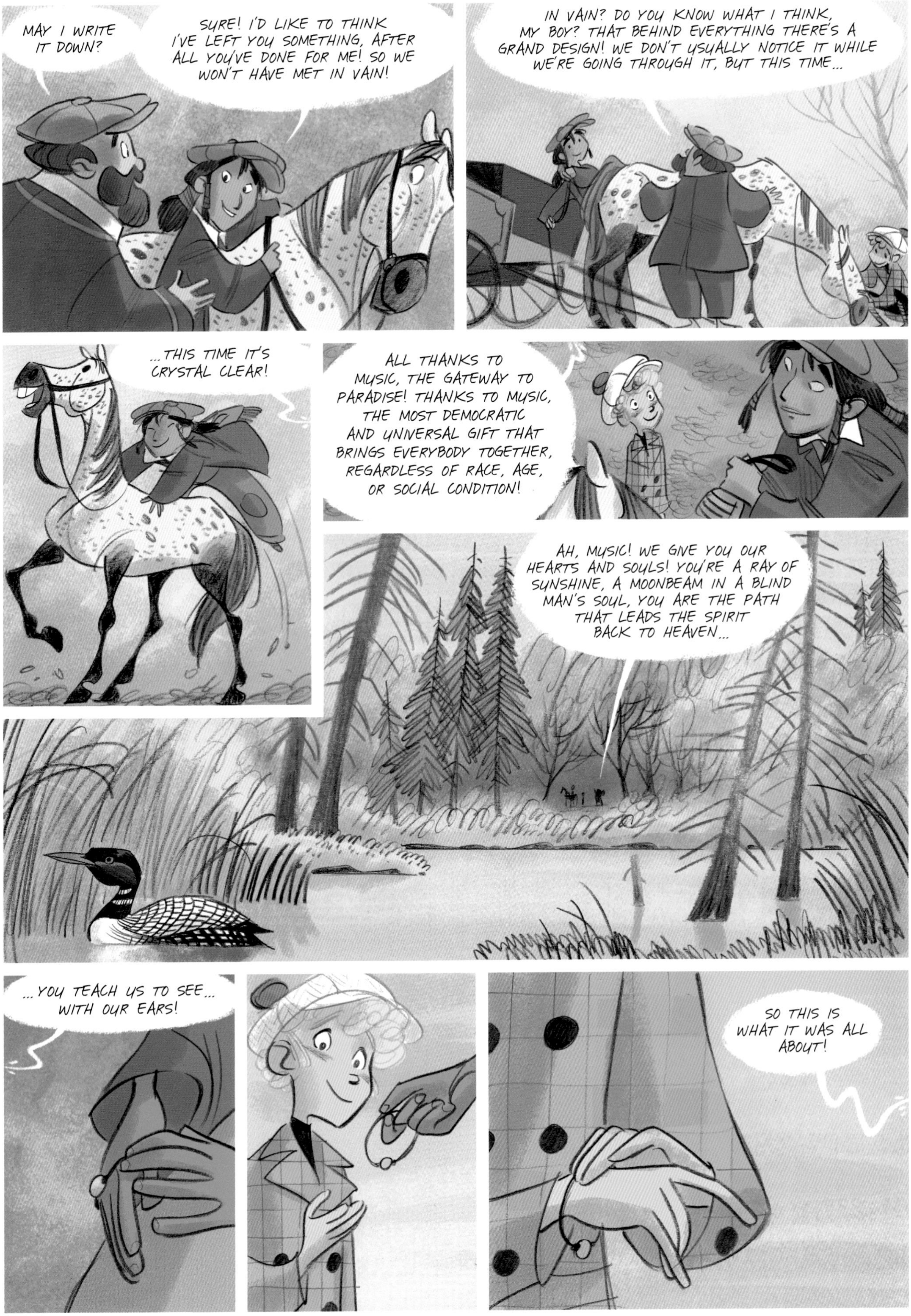
MAY I WRITE IT DOWN?
SURE! I'D LIKE TO THINK I'VE LEFT YOU SOMETHING, AFTER ALL YOU'VE DONE FOR ME! SO WE WON'T HAVE MET IN VAIN!
IN VAIN? DO YOU KNOW WHAT I THINK, MY BOY? THAT BEHIND EVERYTHING THERE'S A GRAND DESIGN! WE DON'T USUALLY NOTICE IT WHILE WE'RE GOING THROUGH IT, BUT THIS TIME...
...THIS TIME IT'S CRYSTAL CLEAR!
ALL THANKS TO MUSIC, THE GATEWAY TO PARADISE! THANKS TO MUSIC, THE MOST DEMOCRATIC AND UNIVERSAL GIFT THAT BRINGS EVERYBODY TOGETHER, REGARDLESS OF RACE, AGE, OR SOCIAL CONDITION!
AH, MUSIC! WE GIVE YOU OUR HEARTS AND SOULS! YOU'RE A RAY OF SUNSHINE, A MOONBEAM IN A BLIND MAN'S SOUL, YOU ARE THE PATH THAT LEADS THE SPIRIT BACK TO HEAVEN...
...YOU TEACH US TO SEE... WITH OUR EARS!
SO THIS IS WHAT IT WAS ALL ABOUT!

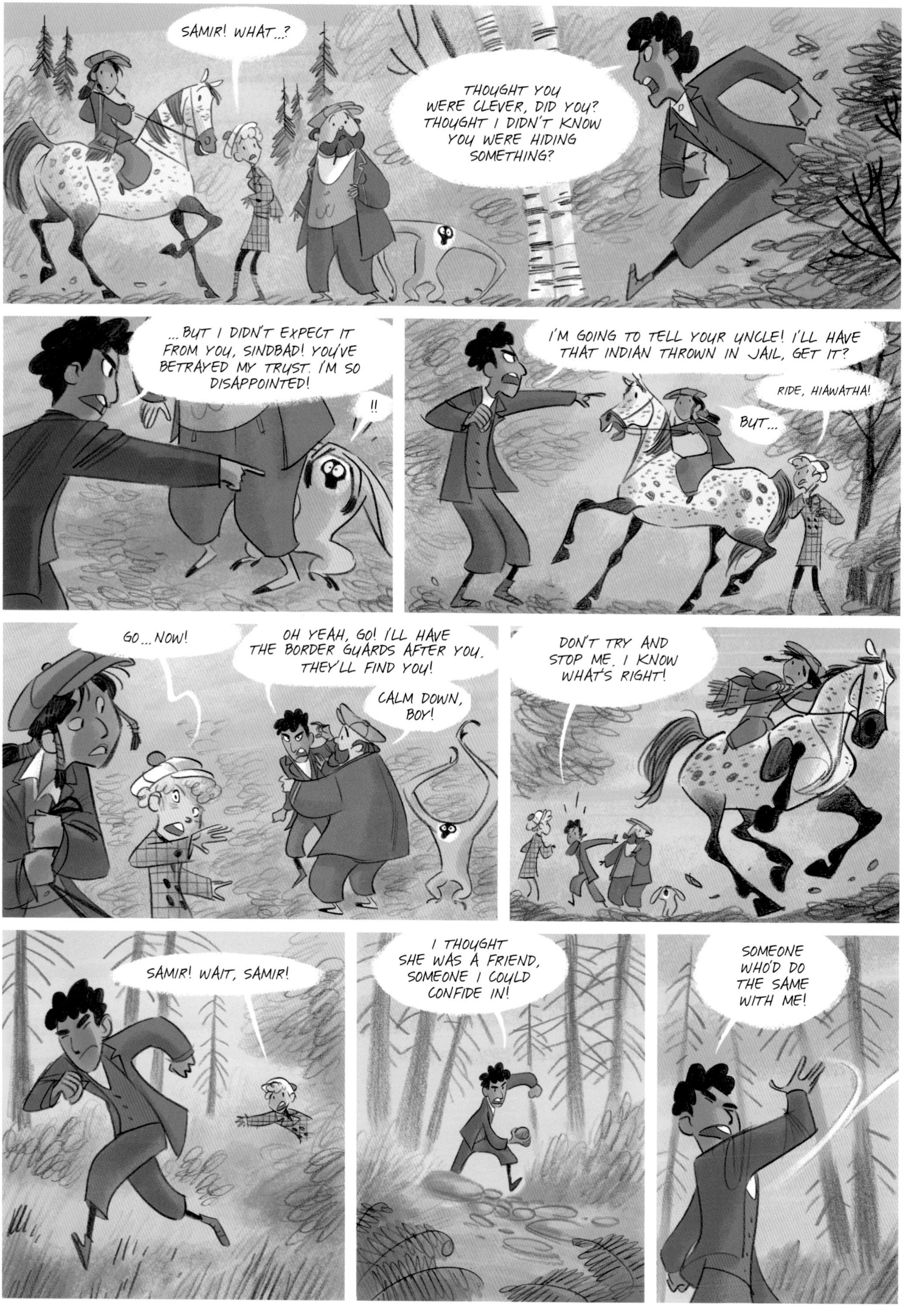
SAMIR! WHAT...?
THOUGHT YOU WERE CLEVER, DID YOU? THOUGHT I DIDN'T KNOW YOU WERE HIDING SOMETHING?
...BUT I DIDN'T EXPECT IT FROM YOU, SINDBAD! YOU'VE BETRAYED MY TRUST. I'M SO DISAPPOINTED!
!!
I'M GOING TO TELL YOUR UNCLE! I'LL HAVE THAT INDIAN THROWN IN JAIL, GET IT?
RIDE, HIAWATHA!
BUT...
GO... NOW!
OH YEAH, GO! I'LL HAVE THE BORDER GUARDS AFTER YOU. THEY'LL FIND YOU!
CALM DOWN, BOY!
DON'T TRY AND STOP ME. I KNOW WHAT'S RIGHT!
!
SAMIR! WAIT, SAMIR!
I THOUGHT SHE WAS A FRIEND, SOMEONE I COULD CONFIDE IN!
SOMEONE WHO'D DO THE SAME WITH ME!

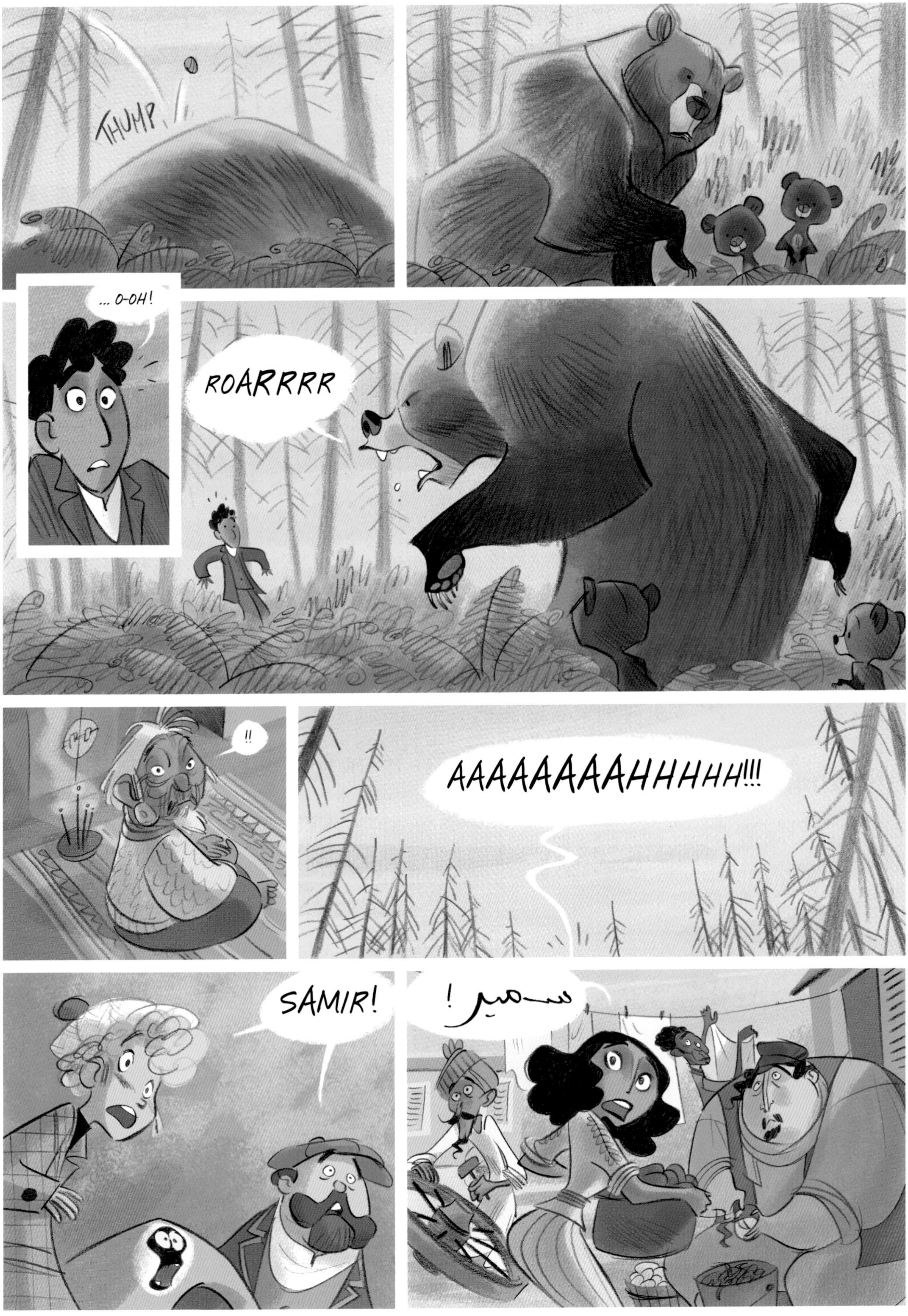
THUMP
... O-OH!
ROARRRR
!!
AAAAAAAAHHHHH!!!
SAMIR!
سمير!

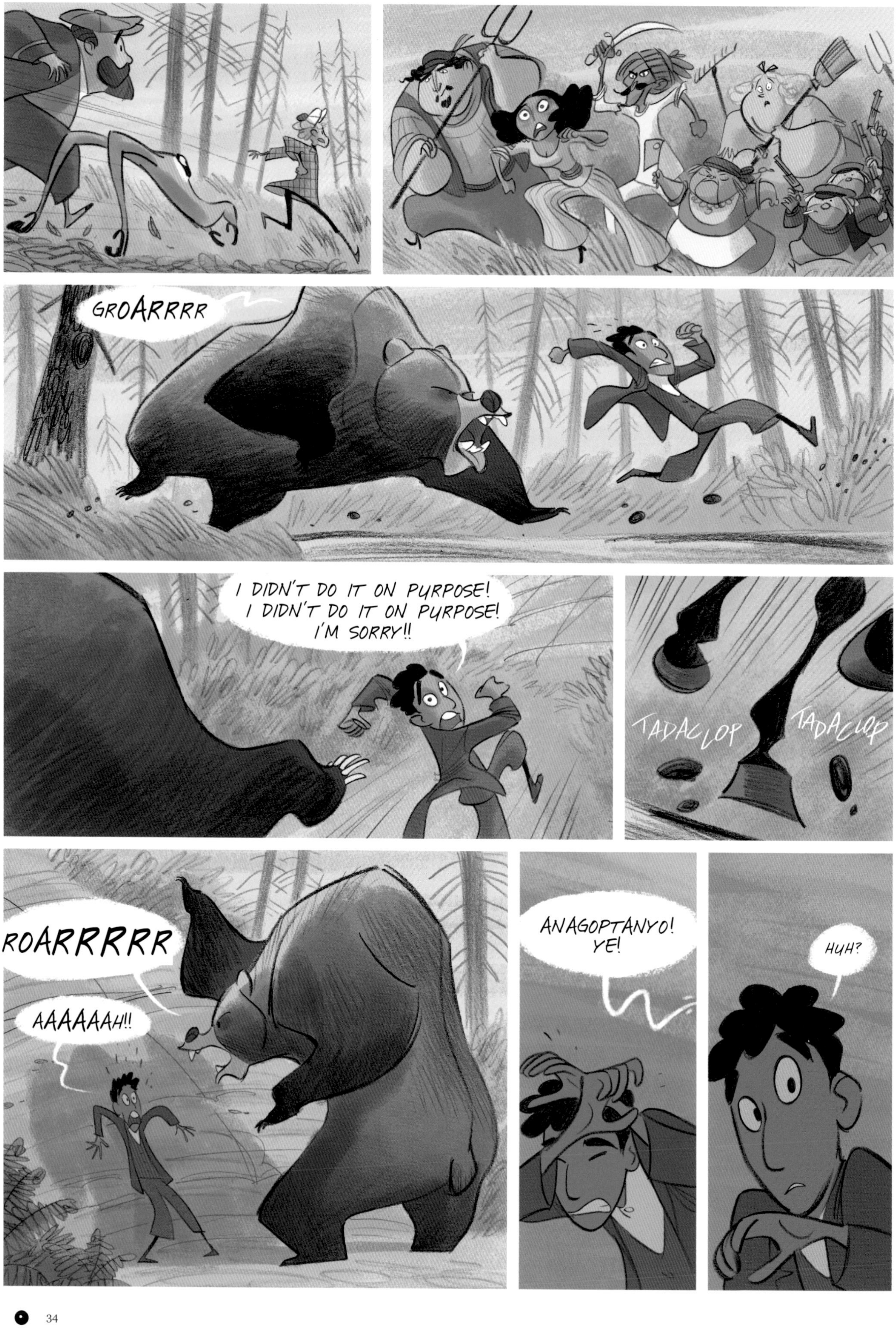
GROARRRR
I DIDN'T DO IT ON PURPOSE!
I DIDN'T DO IT ON PURPOSE!
I'M SORRY!!
TADACLOP
TADACLOP
ROARRRRR
AAAAAAH!!
ANAGOPTANYO!
YE!
HUH?

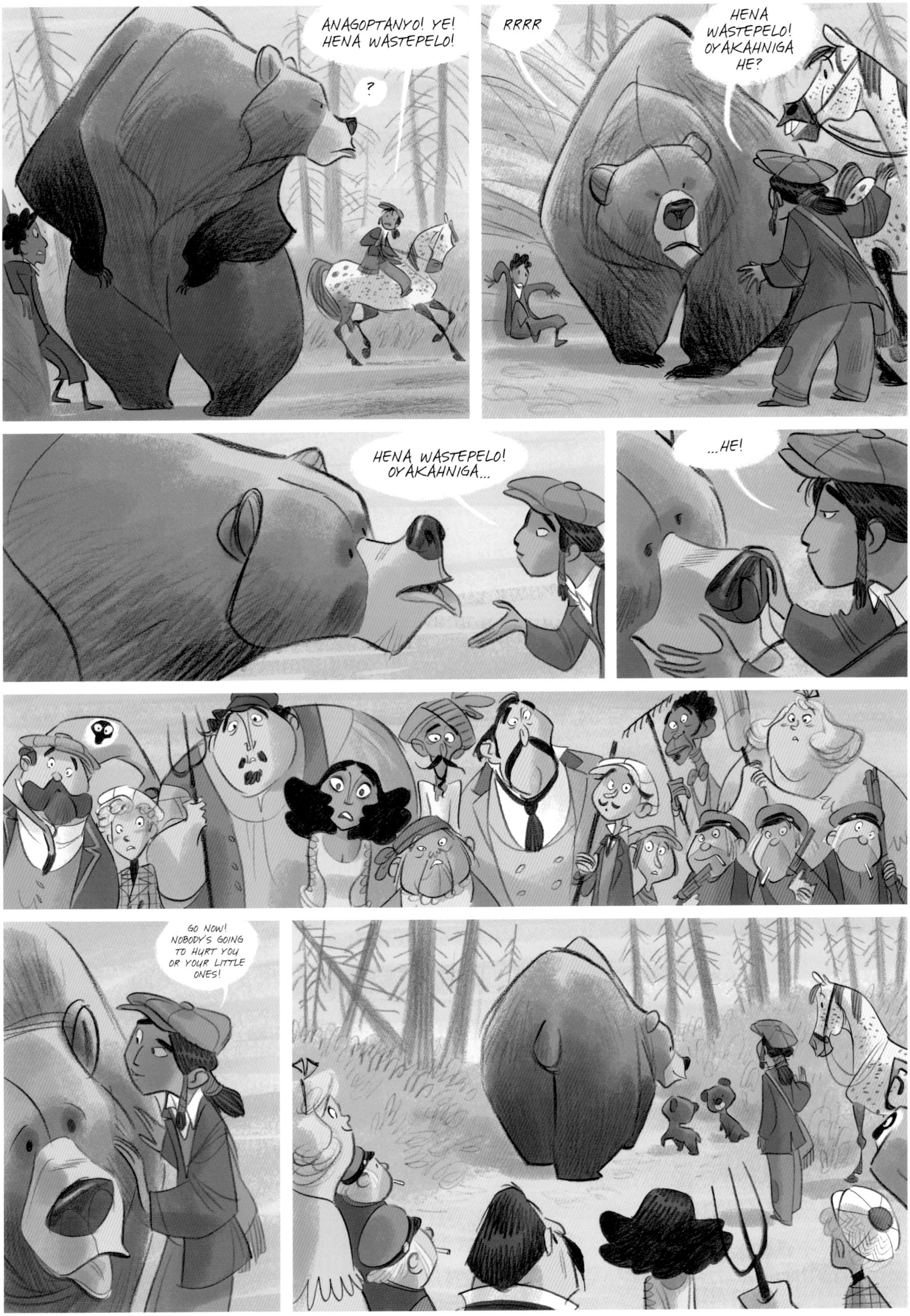
ANAGOPTANYO! YE! HENA WASTEPELO!
?
RRRR
HENA WASTEPELO! OYAKAHNIGA HE?
HENA WASTEPELO! OYAKAHNIGA...
...HE!
GO NOW! NOBODY'S GOING TO HURT YOU OR YOUR LITTLE ONES!

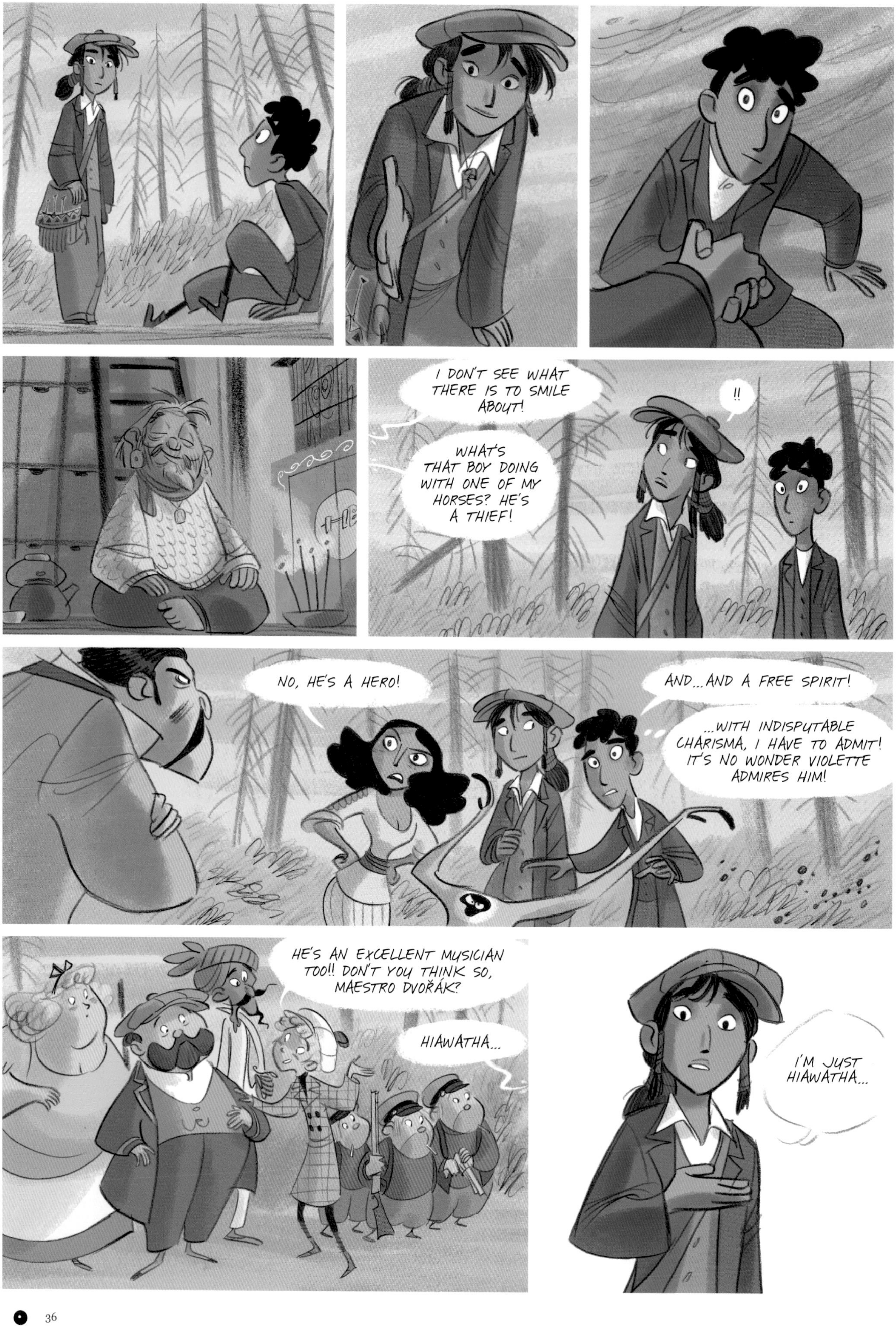
I DON'T SEE WHAT THERE IS TO SMILE ABOUT!
WHAT'S THAT BOY DOING WITH ONE OF MY HORSES? HE'S A THIEF!
!!
NO, HE'S A HERO!
AND... AND A FREE SPIRIT!
...WITH INDISPUTABLE CHARISMA, I HAVE TO ADMIT! IT'S NO WONDER VIOLETTE ADMIRES HIM!
HE'S AN EXCELLENT MUSICIAN TOO!! DON'T YOU THINK SO, MAESTRO DVOŘÁK?
HIAWATHA...
I'M JUST HIAWATHA...

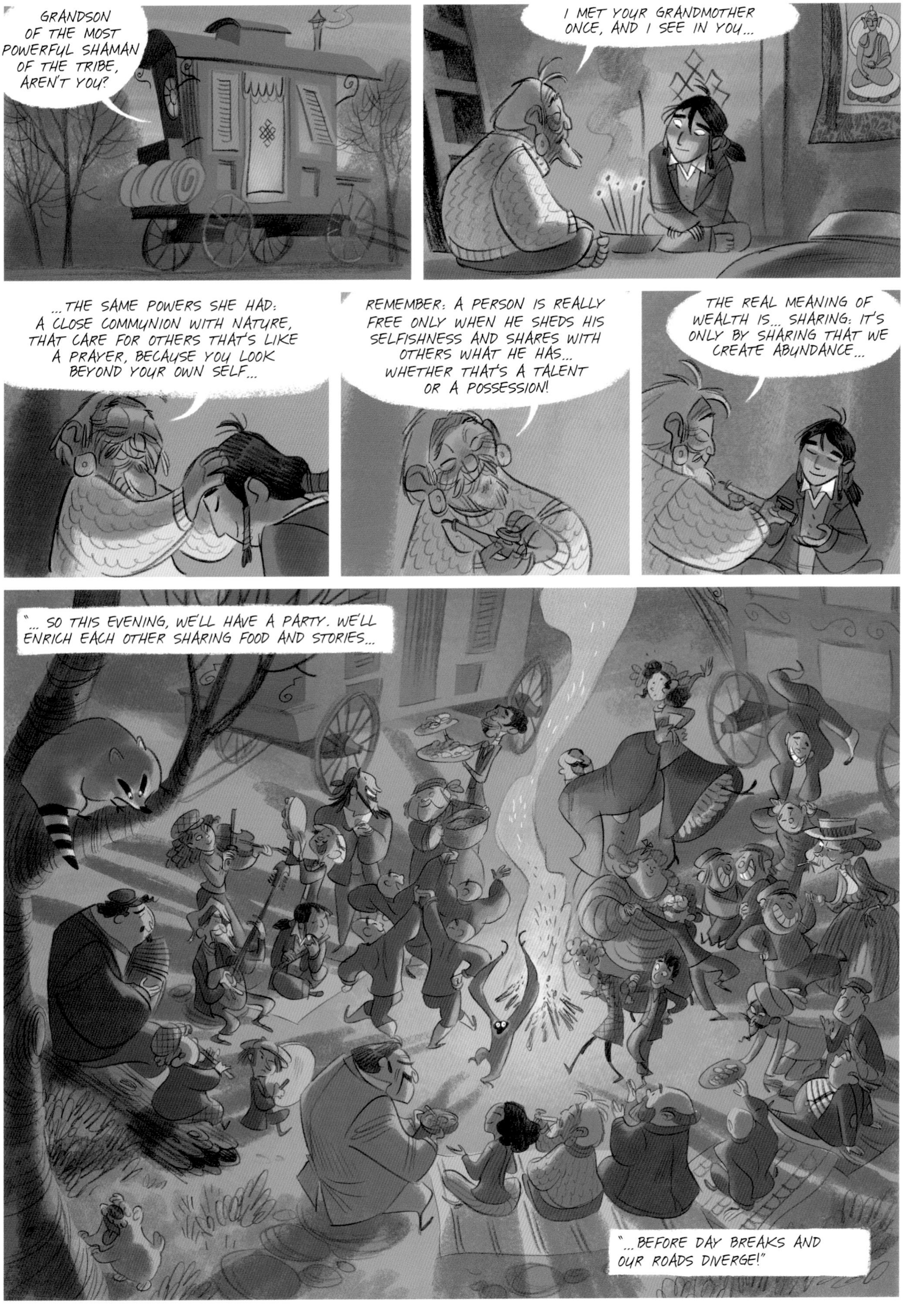
GRANDSON OF THE MOST POWERFUL SHAMAN OF THE TRIBE, AREN'T YOU?
I MET YOUR GRANDMOTHER ONCE, AND I SEE IN YOU...
...THE SAME POWERS SHE HAD: A CLOSE COMMUNION WITH NATURE, THAT CARE FOR OTHERS THAT'S LIKE A PRAYER, BECAUSE YOU LOOK BEYOND YOUR OWN SELF...
REMEMBER: A PERSON IS REALLY FREE ONLY WHEN HE SHEDS HIS SELFISHNESS AND SHARES WITH OTHERS WHAT HE HAS... WHETHER THAT'S A TALENT OR A POSSESSION!
THE REAL MEANING OF WEALTH IS... SHARING: IT'S ONLY BY SHARING THAT WE CREATE ABUNDANCE...
"... SO THIS EVENING, WE'LL HAVE A PARTY. WE'LL ENRICH EACH OTHER SHARING FOOD AND STORIES...
"... BEFORE DAY BREAKS AND OUR ROADS DIVERGE!"

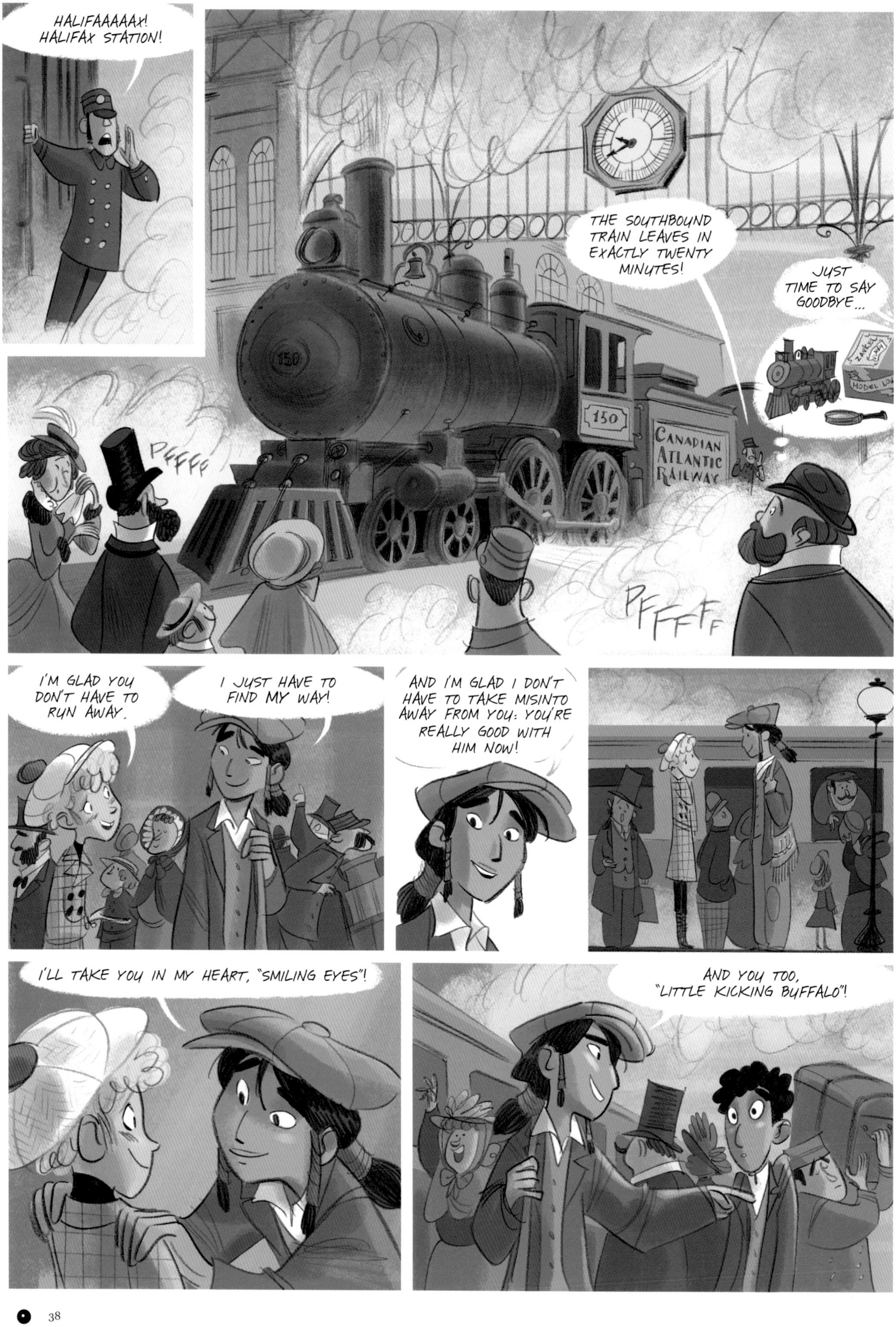
HALIFAAAAAX! HALIFAX STATION!
THE SOUTHBOUND TRAIN LEAVES IN EXACTLY TWENTY MINUTES!
JUST TIME TO SAY GOODBYE...
150
150
CANADIAN ATLANTIC RAILWAY
PFFFF
PFFFFF
I'M GLAD YOU DON'T HAVE TO RUN AWAY.
I JUST HAVE TO FIND MY WAY!
AND I'M GLAD I DON'T HAVE TO TAKE MISINTO AWAY FROM YOU: YOU'RE REALLY GOOD WITH HIM NOW!
I'LL TAKE YOU IN MY HEART, "SMILING EYES"!
AND YOU TOO, "LITTLE KICKING BUFFALO"!

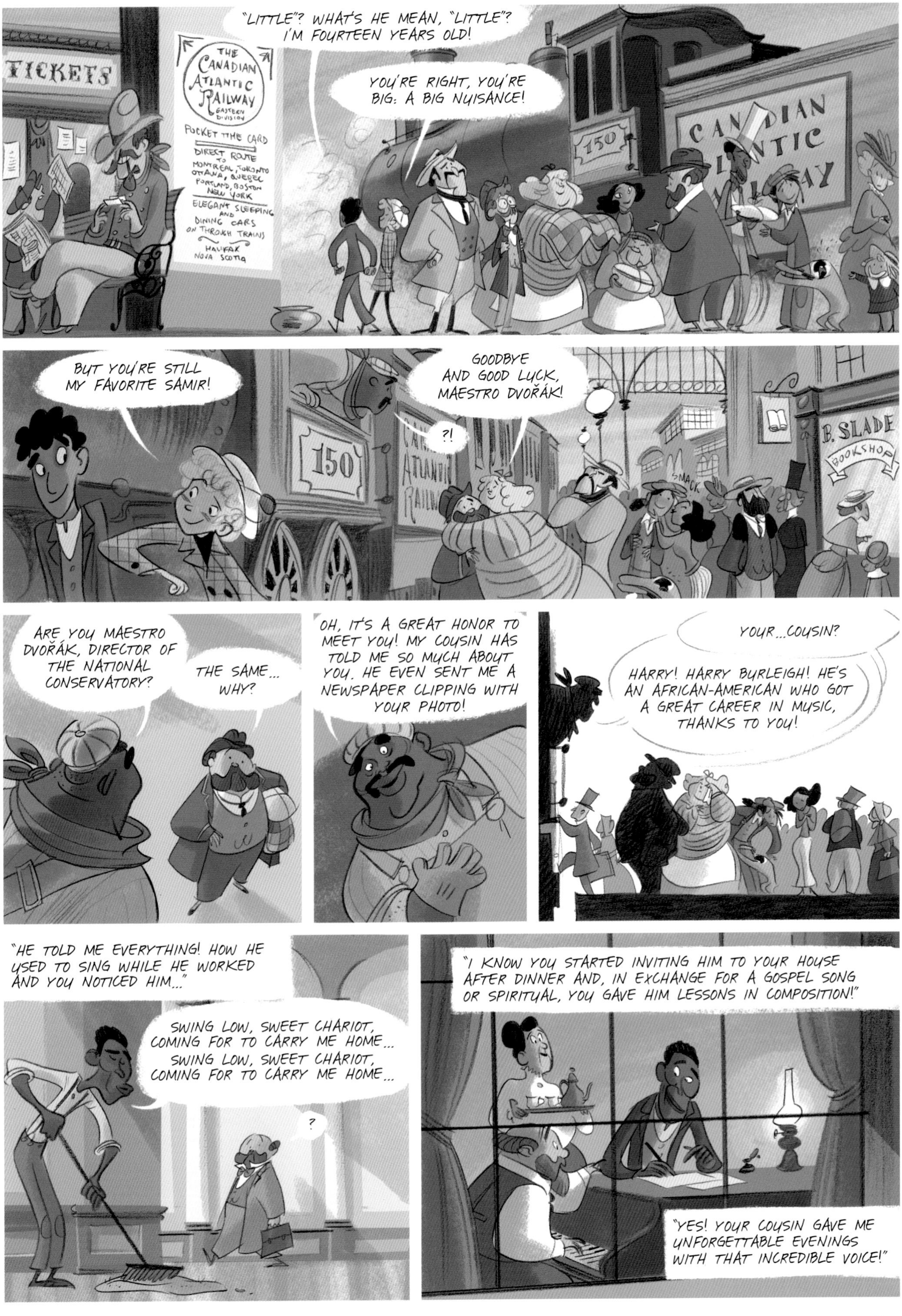
TICKETS
THE CANADIAN ATLANTIC RAILWAY
EASTERN DIVISION
POCKET THE CARD
DIRECT ROUTE TO MONTREAL, TORONTO OTTAWA, QUEBEC PORTLAND, BOSTON NEW YORK
ELEGANT SLEEPING AND DINING CARS ON THROUGH TRAINS
HALIFAX NOVA SCOTIA
"LITTLE"? WHAT'S HE MEAN, "LITTLE"? I'M FOURTEEN YEARS OLD!
YOU'RE RIGHT, YOU'RE BIG: A BIG NUISANCE!
150
CANADIAN ATLANTIC RAILWAY
BUT YOU'RE STILL MY FAVORITE SAMIR!
GOODBYE AND GOOD LUCK, MAESTRO DVOŘÁK!
?!
150
SMACK
B. SLADE
BOOKSHOP
ARE YOU MAESTRO DVOŘÁK, DIRECTOR OF THE NATIONAL CONSERVATORY?
THE SAME... WHY?
OH, IT'S A GREAT HONOR TO MEET YOU! MY COUSIN HAS TOLD ME SO MUCH ABOUT YOU. HE EVEN SENT ME A NEWSPAPER CLIPPING WITH YOUR PHOTO!
YOUR...COUSIN?
HARRY! HARRY BURLEIGH! HE'S AN AFRICAN-AMERICAN WHO GOT A GREAT CAREER IN MUSIC, THANKS TO YOU!
"HE TOLD ME EVERYTHING! HOW HE USED TO SING WHILE HE WORKED AND YOU NOTICED HIM..."
SWING LOW, SWEET CHARIOT, COMING FOR TO CARRY ME HOME... SWING LOW, SWEET CHARIOT, COMING FOR TO CARRY ME HOME...
?
"I KNOW YOU STARTED INVITING HIM TO YOUR HOUSE AFTER DINNER AND, IN EXCHANGE FOR A GOSPEL SONG OR SPIRITUAL, YOU GAVE HIM LESSONS IN COMPOSITION!"
"YES! YOUR COUSIN GAVE ME UNFORGETTABLE EVENINGS WITH THAT INCREDIBLE VOICE!"

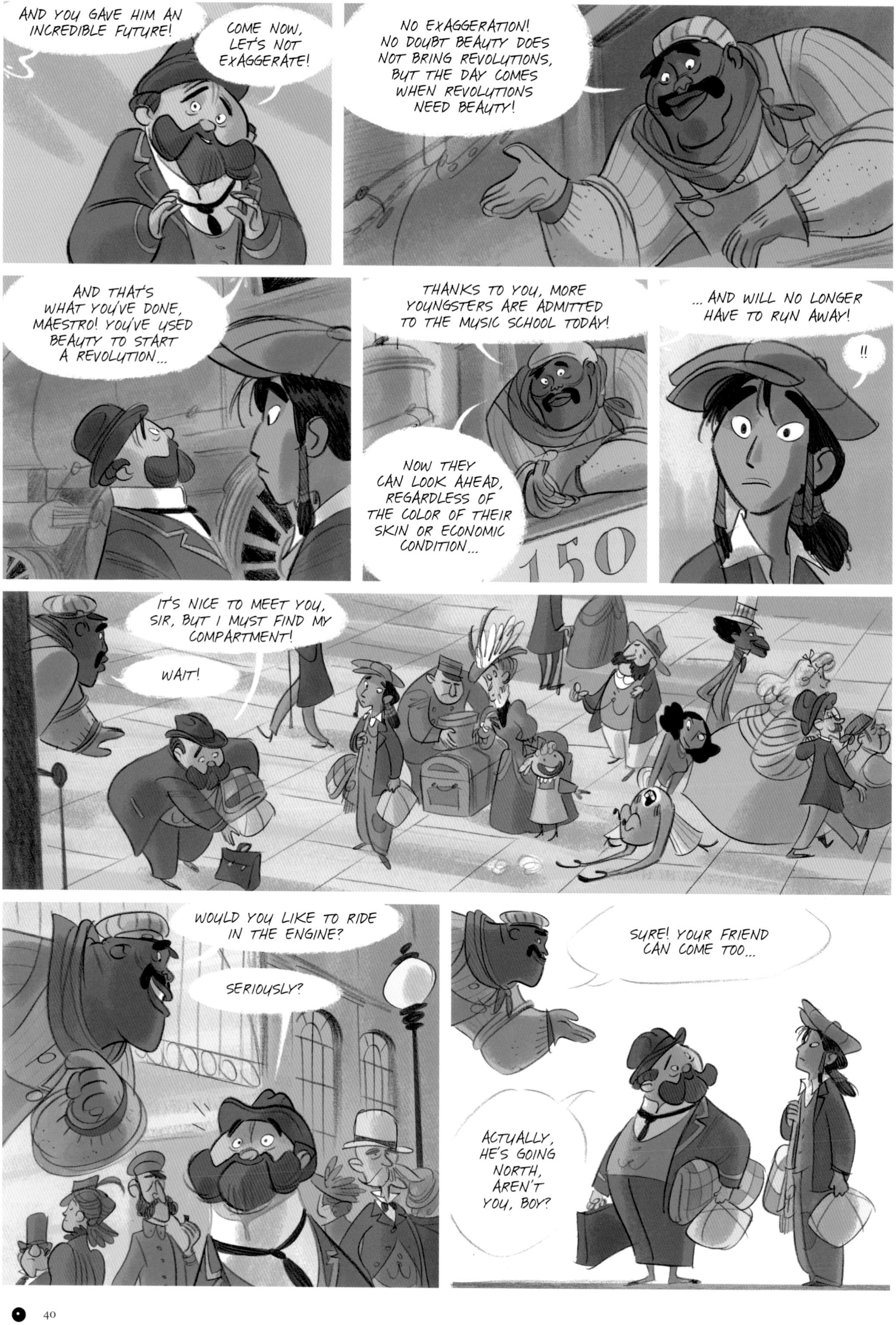
AND YOU GAVE HIM AN INCREDIBLE FUTURE!
COME NOW, LET'S NOT EXAGGERATE!
NO EXAGGERATION! NO DOUBT BEAUTY DOES NOT BRING REVOLUTIONS, BUT THE DAY COMES WHEN REVOLUTIONS NEED BEAUTY!
AND THAT'S WHAT YOU'VE DONE, MAESTRO! YOU'VE USED BEAUTY TO START A REVOLUTION...
THANKS TO YOU, MORE YOUNGSTERS ARE ADMITTED TO THE MUSIC SCHOOL TODAY!
NOW THEY CAN LOOK AHEAD, REGARDLESS OF THE COLOR OF THEIR SKIN OR ECONOMIC CONDITION...
150
... AND WILL NO LONGER HAVE TO RUN AWAY!
!!
IT'S NICE TO MEET YOU, SIR, BUT I MUST FIND MY COMPARTMENT!
WAIT!
WOULD YOU LIKE TO RIDE IN THE ENGINE?
SERIOUSLY?
SURE! YOUR FRIEND CAN COME TOO...
ACTUALLY, HE'S GOING NORTH, AREN'T YOU, BOY?

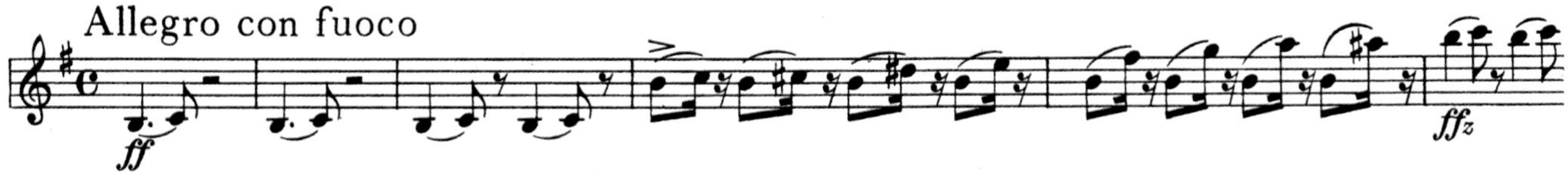
Allegro con fuoco
ff
ffz

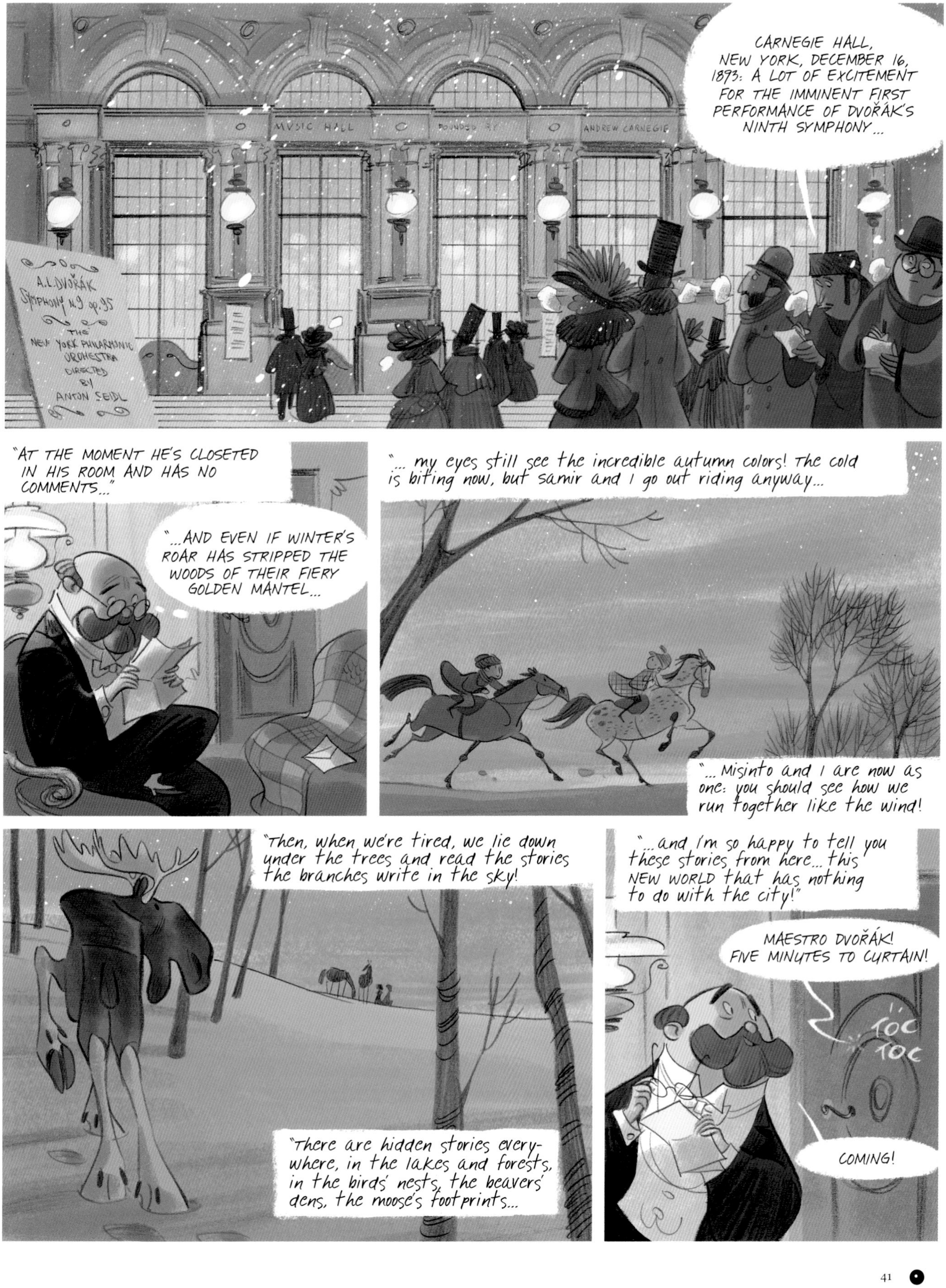
MUSIC HALL
FOUNDED BY
ANDREW CARNEGIE
A.L. DVOŘÁK
SYMPHONY N.9 op.95
THE NEW YORK PHILHARMONIC ORCHESTRA
DIRECTED BY
ANTON SEIDL
CARNEGIE HALL, NEW YORK, DECEMBER 16, 1893: A LOT OF EXCITEMENT FOR THE IMMINENT FIRST PERFORMANCE OF DVOŘÁK'S NINTH SYMPHONY...
"AT THE MOMENT HE'S CLOSETED IN HIS ROOM AND HAS NO COMMENTS..."
"...AND EVEN IF WINTER'S ROAR HAS STRIPPED THE WOODS OF THEIR FIERY GOLDEN MANTEL...
"... my eyes still see the incredible autumn colors! The cold is biting now, but Samir and I go out riding anyway...
"... Misinto and I are now as one: you should see how we run together like the wind!
"Then, when we're tired, we lie down under the trees and read the stories the branches write in the sky!
"There are hidden stories everywhere, in the lakes and forests, in the birds' nests, the beavers' dens, the moose's footprints...
"... and I'm so happy to tell you these stories from here... this NEW WORLD that has nothing to do with the city!"
MAESTRO DVOŘÁK! FIVE MINUTES TO CURTAIN!
TOC TOC
COMING!

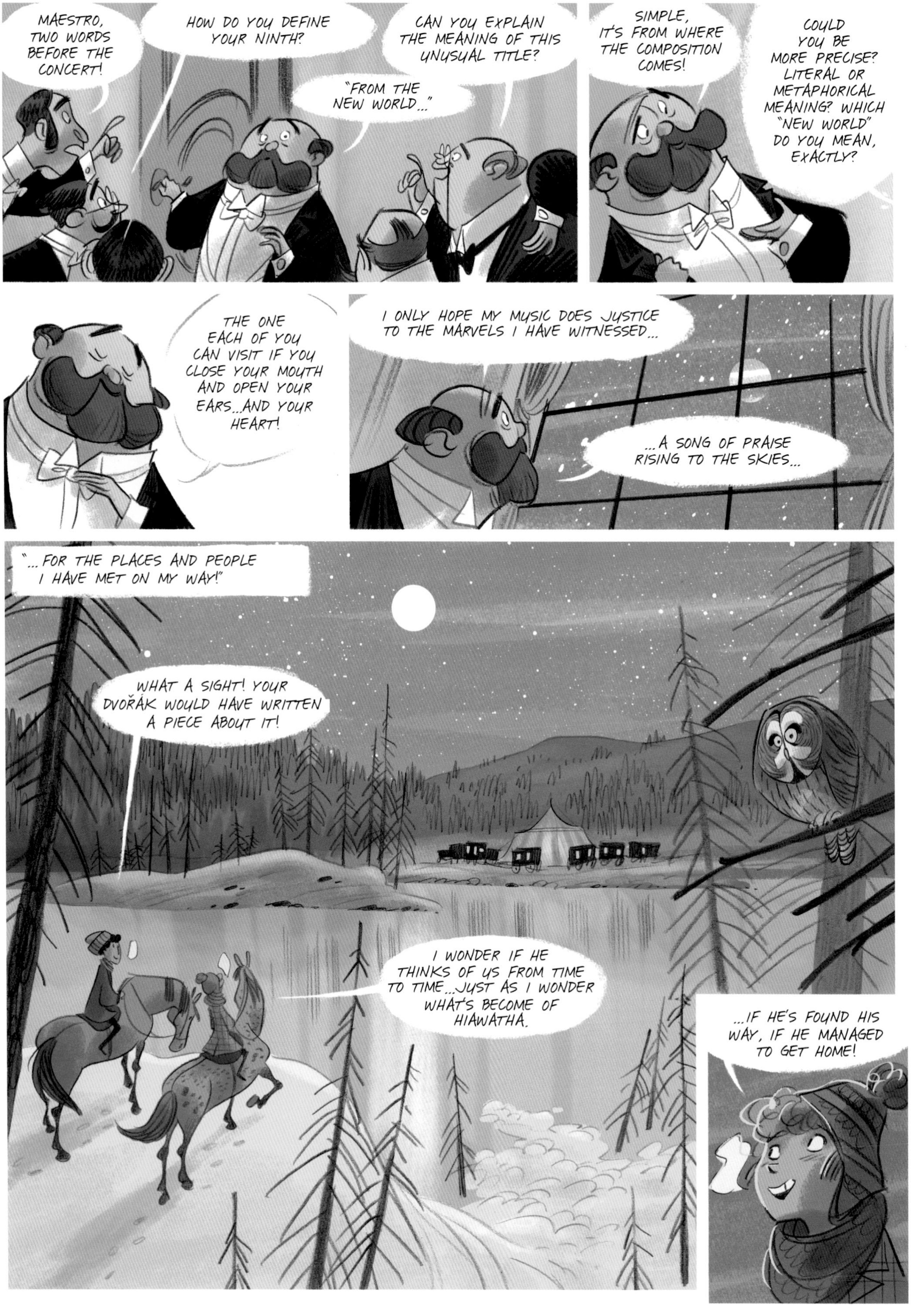
MAESTRO, TWO WORDS BEFORE THE CONCERT!
HOW DO YOU DEFINE YOUR NINTH?
CAN YOU EXPLAIN THE MEANING OF THIS UNUSUAL TITLE?
"FROM THE NEW WORLD..."
SIMPLE, IT'S FROM WHERE THE COMPOSITION COMES!
COULD YOU BE MORE PRECISE? LITERAL OR METAPHORICAL MEANING? WHICH "NEW WORLD" DO YOU MEAN, EXACTLY?
THE ONE EACH OF YOU CAN VISIT IF YOU CLOSE YOUR MOUTH AND OPEN YOUR EARS...AND YOUR HEART!
I ONLY HOPE MY MUSIC DOES JUSTICE TO THE MARVELS I HAVE WITNESSED...
...A SONG OF PRAISE RISING TO THE SKIES...
"...FOR THE PLACES AND PEOPLE I HAVE MET ON MY WAY!"
WHAT A SIGHT! YOUR DVOŘÁK WOULD HAVE WRITTEN A PIECE ABOUT IT!
I WONDER IF HE THINKS OF US FROM TIME TO TIME...JUST AS I WONDER WHAT'S BECOME OF HIAWATHA.
...IF HE'S FOUND HIS WAY, IF HE MANAGED TO GET HOME!

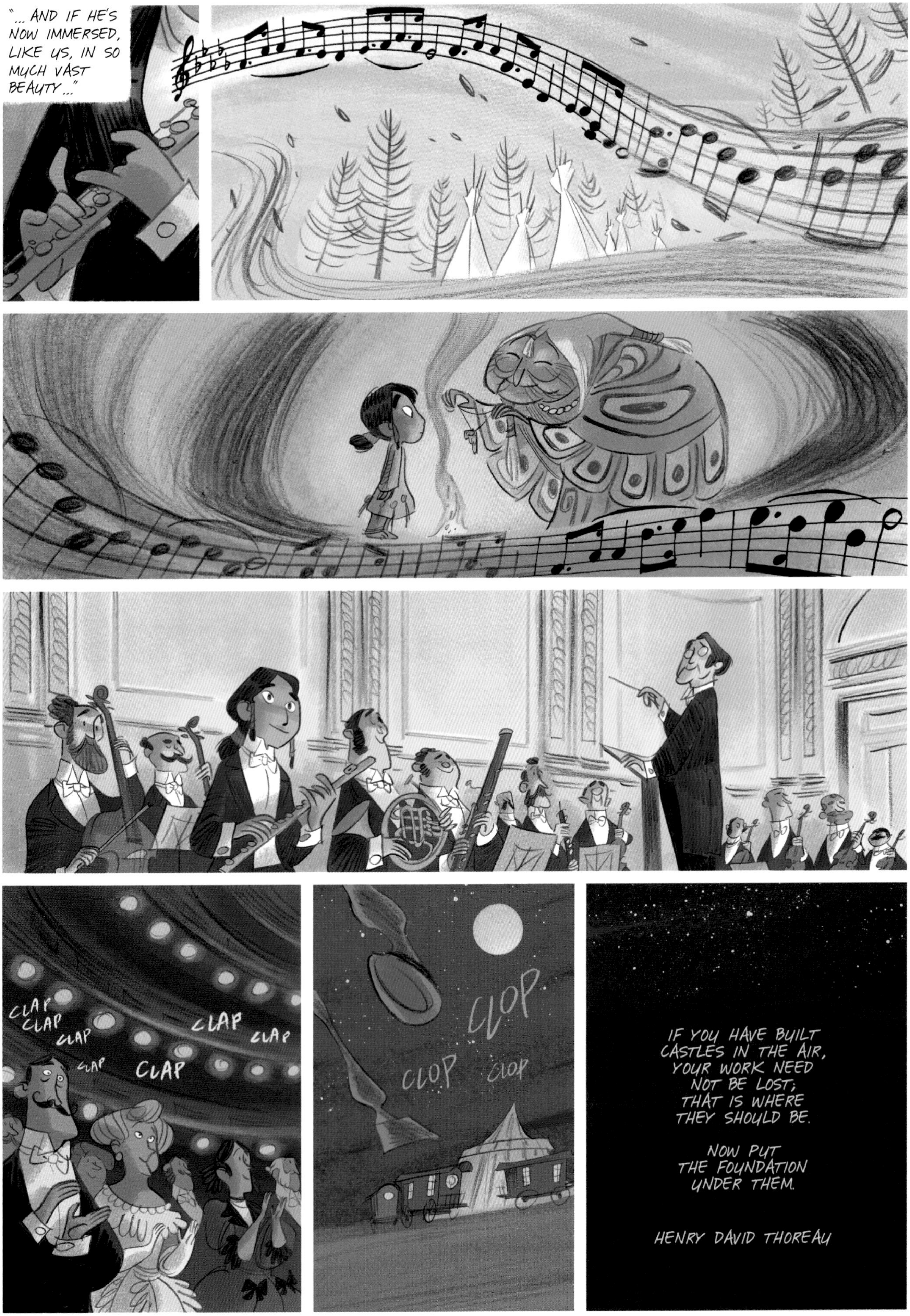
"... AND IF HE'S NOW IMMERSED, LIKE US, IN SO MUCH VAST BEAUTY..."
CLAP CLAP CLAP CLAP CLAP CLAP CLAP
CLOP CLOP CLOP
IF YOU HAVE BUILT CASTLES IN THE AIR, YOUR WORK NEED NOT BE LOST; THAT IS WHERE THEY SHOULD BE.
NOW PUT THE FOUNDATION UNDER THEM.
HENRY DAVID THOREAU

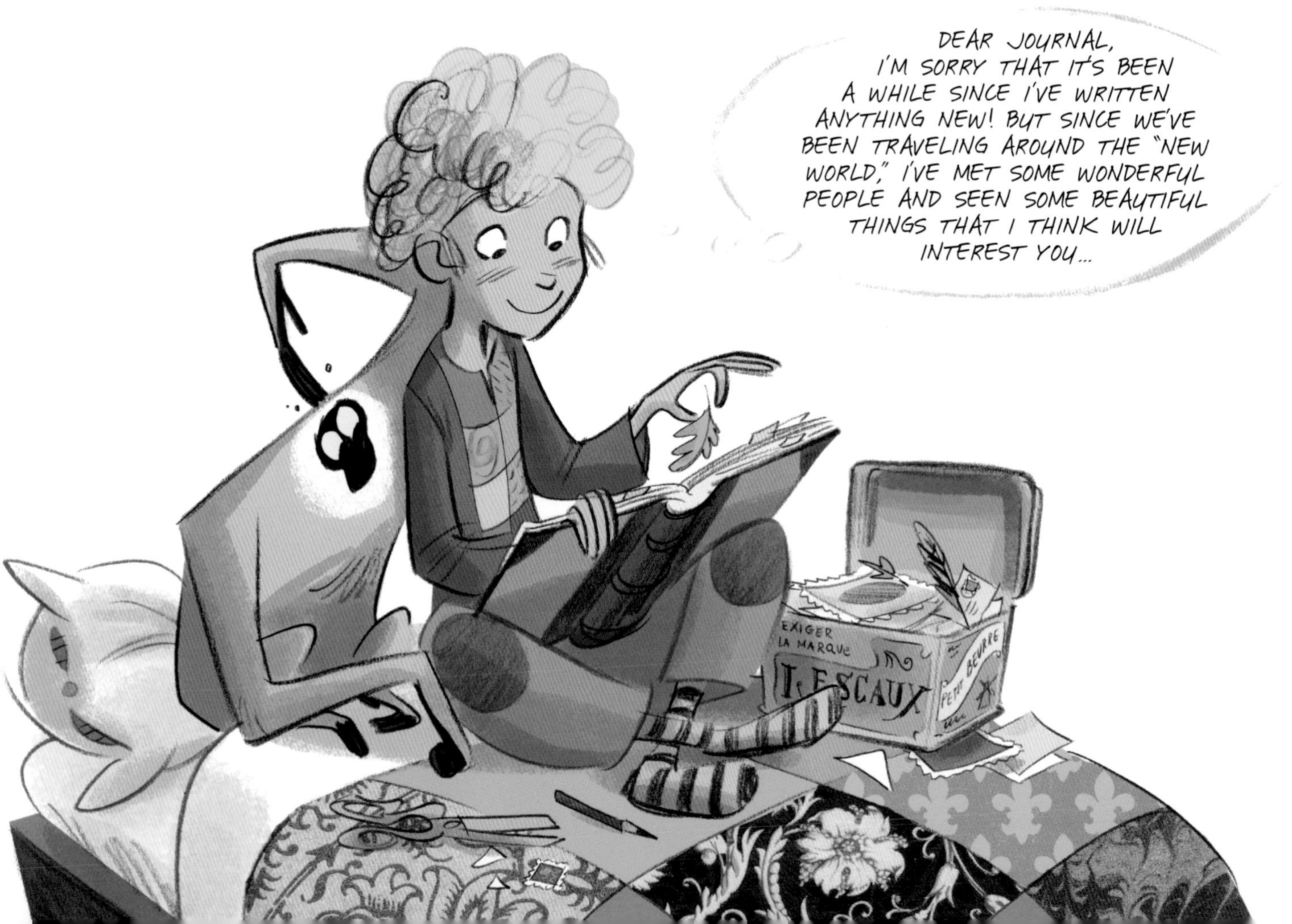
DEAR JOURNAL,
I'M SORRY THAT IT'S BEEN A WHILE SINCE I'VE WRITTEN ANYTHING NEW! BUT SINCE WE'VE BEEN TRAVELING AROUND THE "NEW WORLD," I'VE MET SOME WONDERFUL PEOPLE AND SEEN SOME BEAUTIFUL THINGS THAT I THINK WILL INTEREST YOU...
EXIGER
LA MARQUE
LESCAUX

Antonín Leopold Dvořák

(1841-1904) was a great musician and composer of the 19th Century. He was born in Bohemia (now, the Czech Republic), not far from Prague. He was world renowned and gave concerts in Europe and Russia, then the United States, where he was appointed director of the National Conservatory of Music in New York between 1892 and 1895. While there he created his most famous work: his Symphony No. 9: "From the New World."

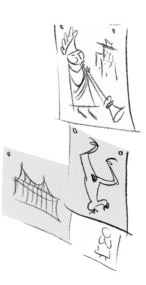

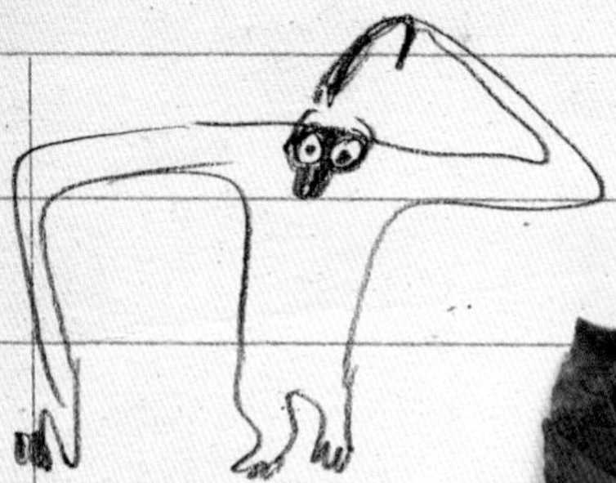

Maple seed pods

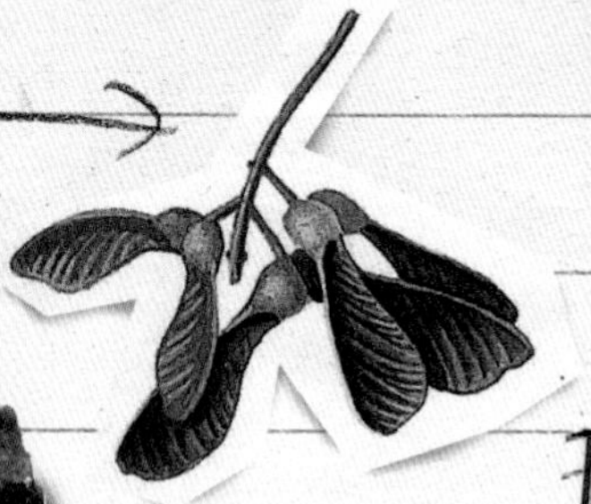

A squirrel eating Arsene's peanuts

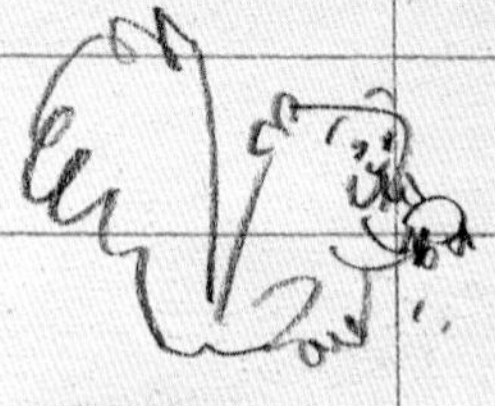

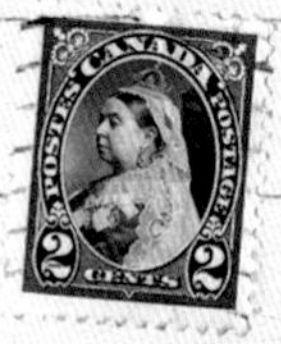
POSTES CANADA POSTAGE
2 CENTS 2

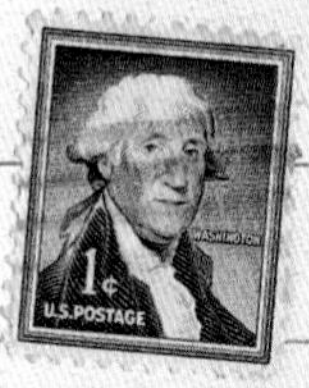
1¢
U.S.POSTAGE

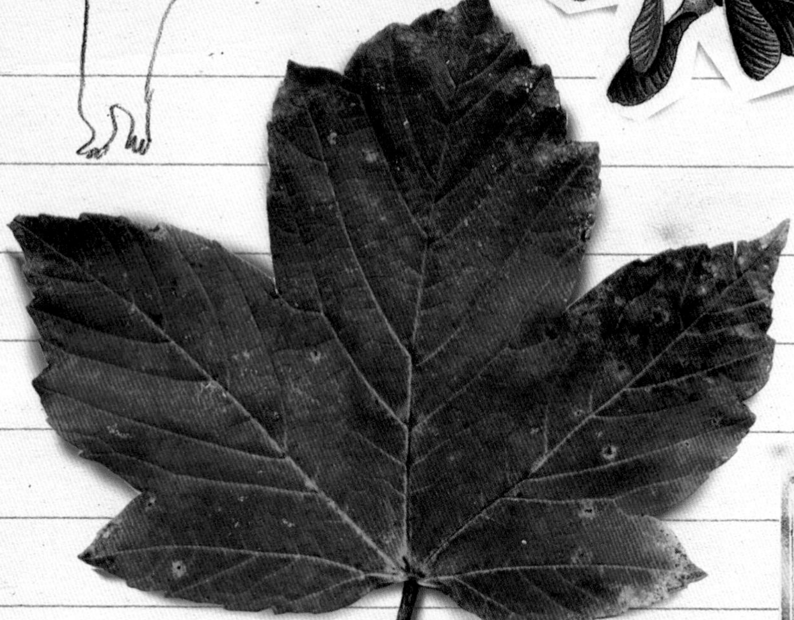

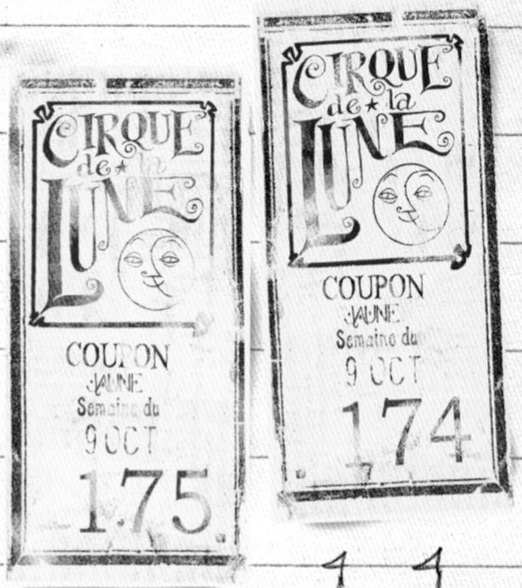
CIRQUE de la LUNE
COUPON
JAUNE
Semaine du
9 OCT
175
CIRQUE de la LUNE
COUPON
JAUNE
Semaine du
9 OCT
174

I just love the beautiful colors of Autumn leaves!

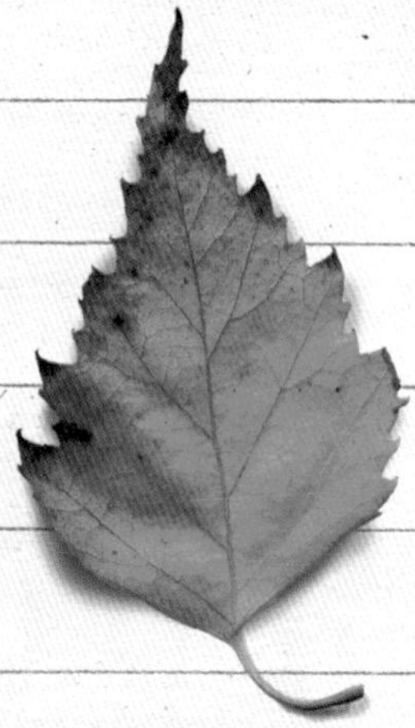

Here are tickets from our first show in Canada

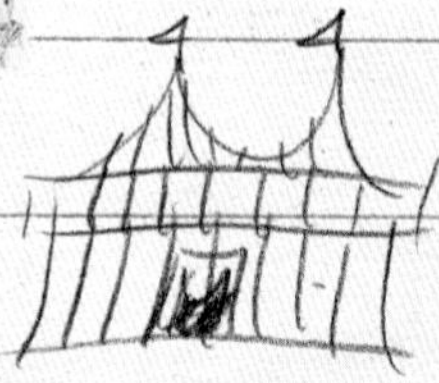

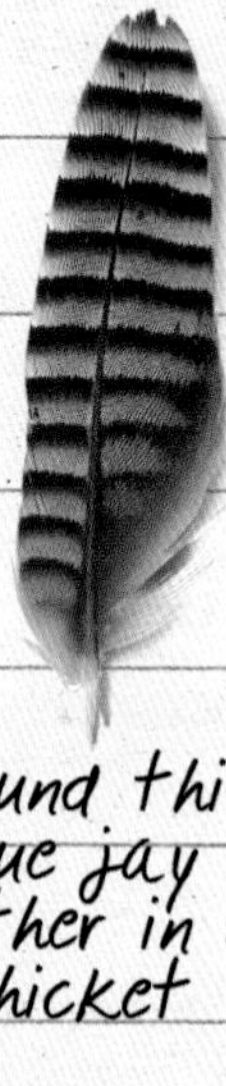

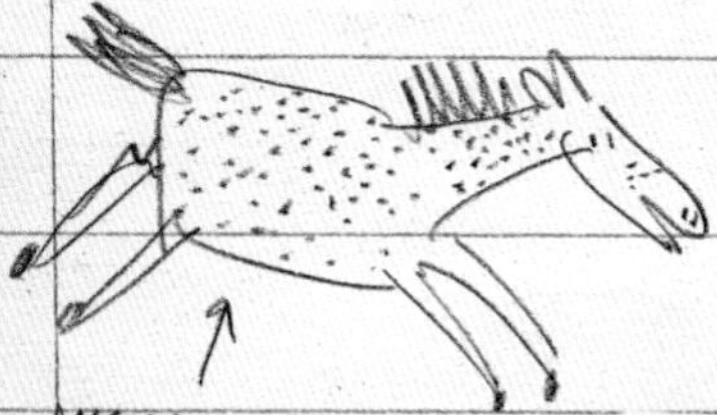

MISINTO

I found this blue jay feather in a thicket

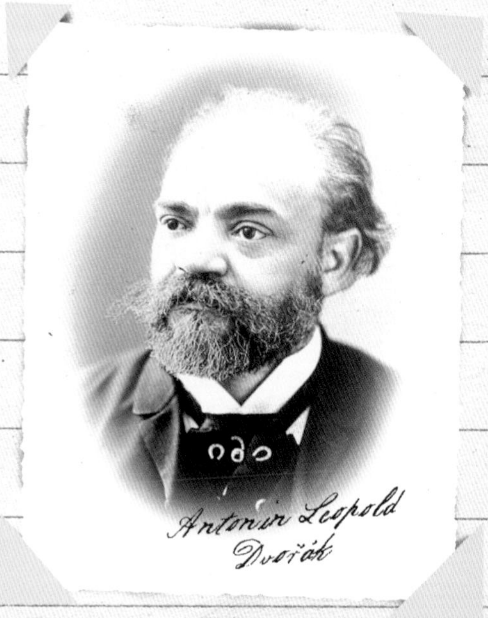
Antonín Leopold Dvořák

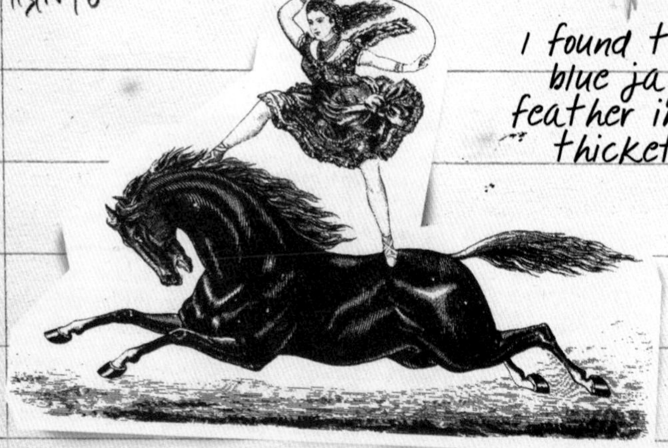

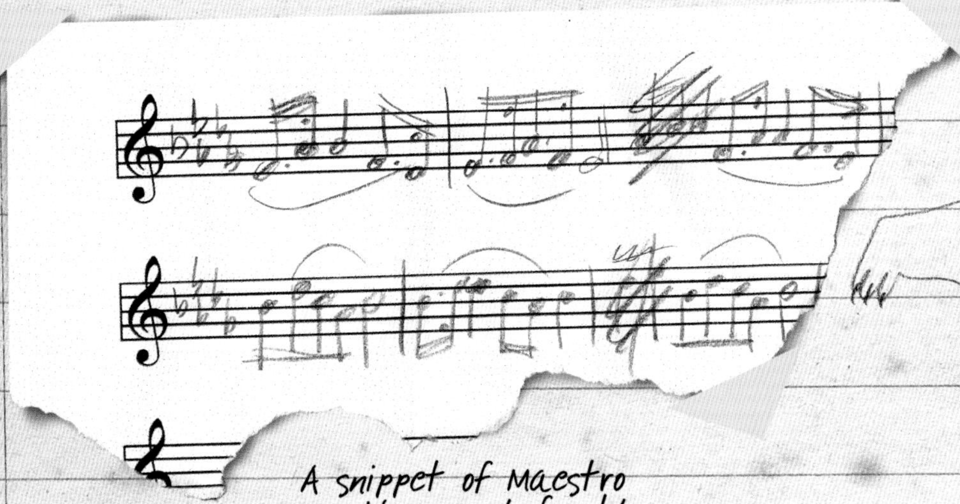

A snippet of Maestro Dvorak's search for the right notes to use in his new symphony

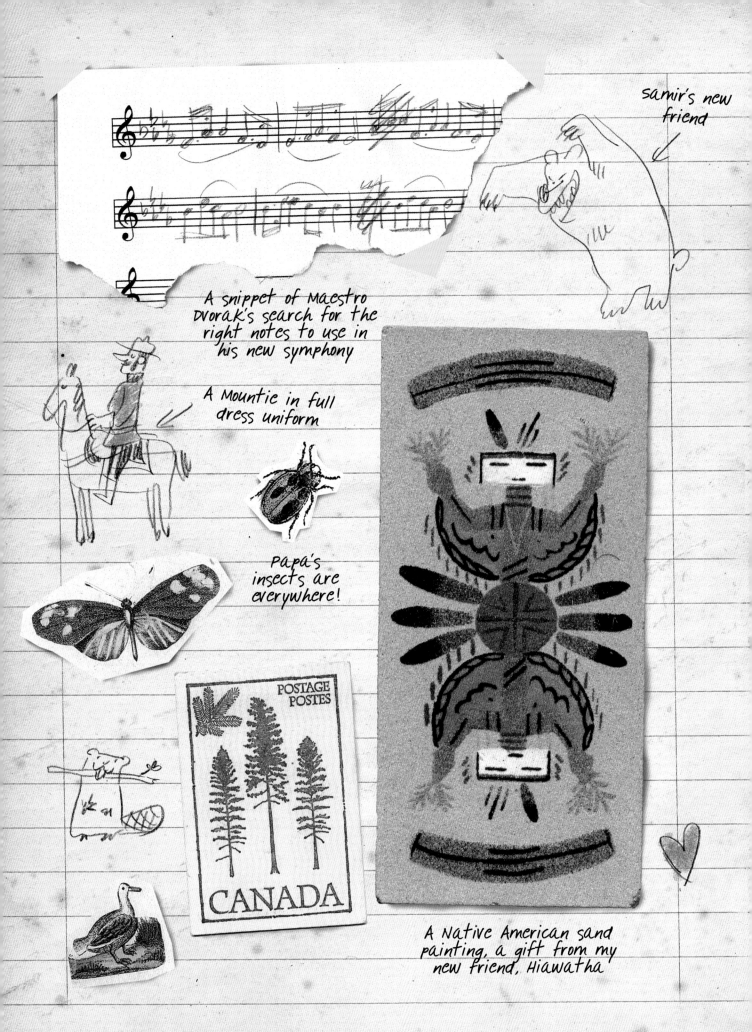

samir's new friend

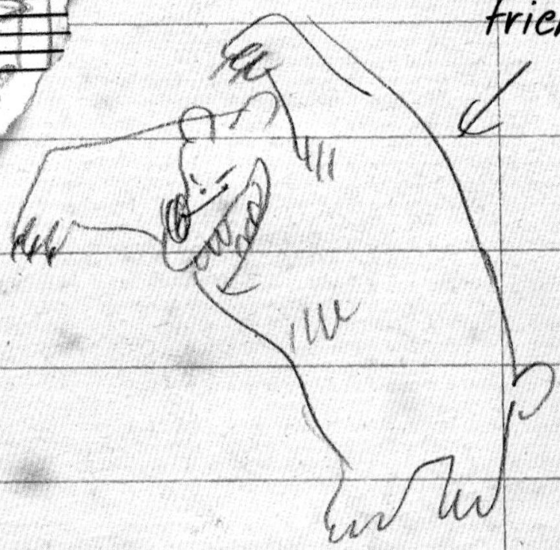

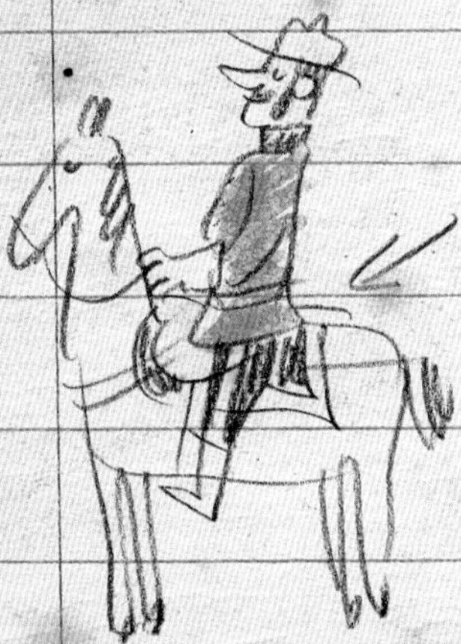

A Mountie in full dress uniform

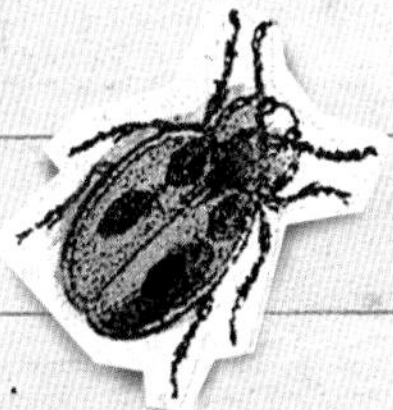

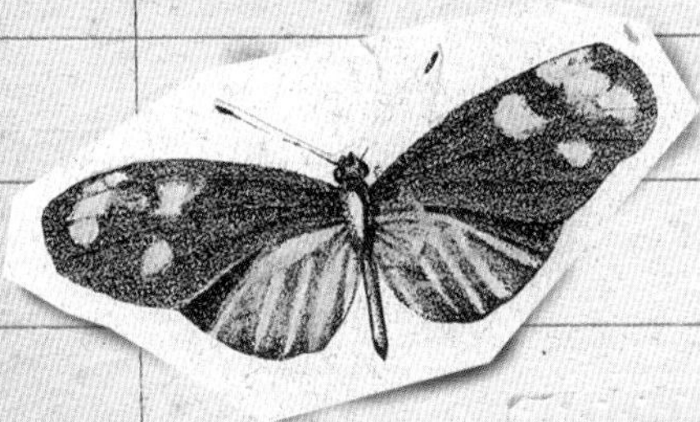

Papa's insects are everywhere!

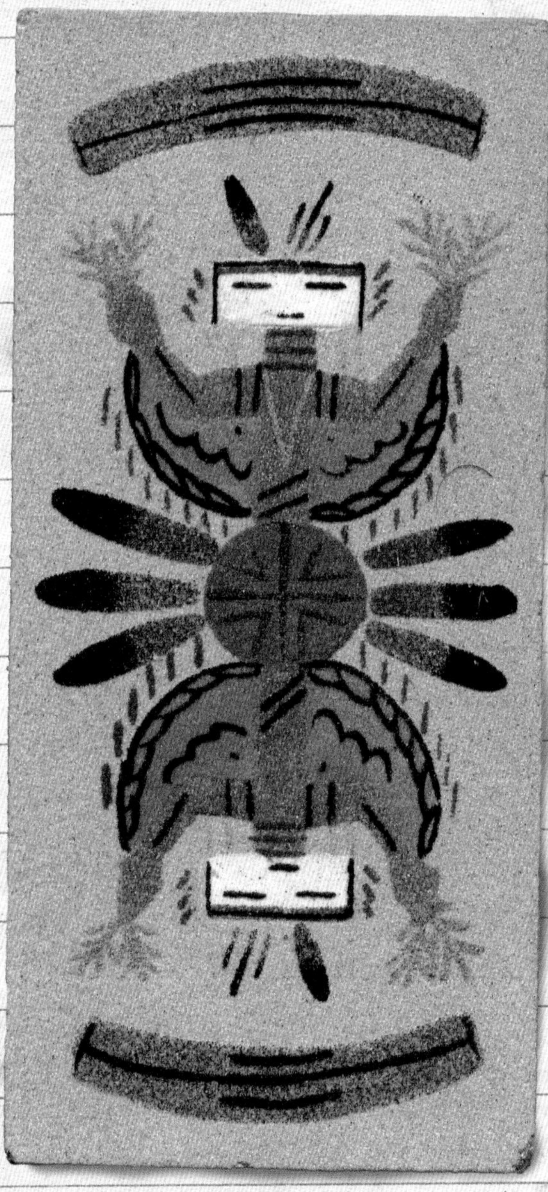

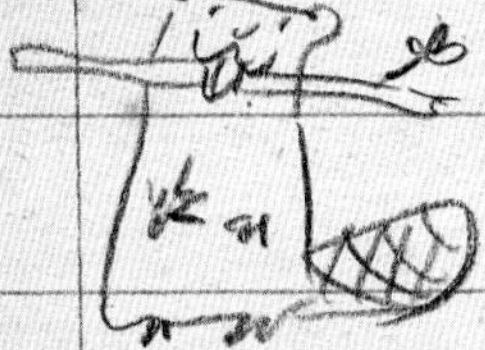

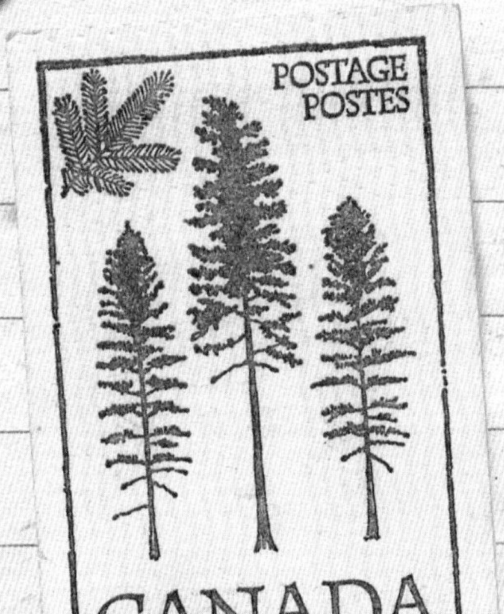
POSTAGE
POSTES
CANADA

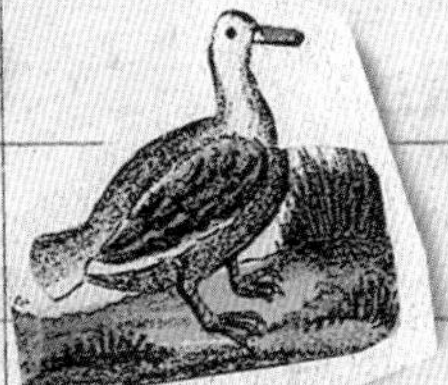

A Native American sand painting, a gift from my new friend, Hiawatha

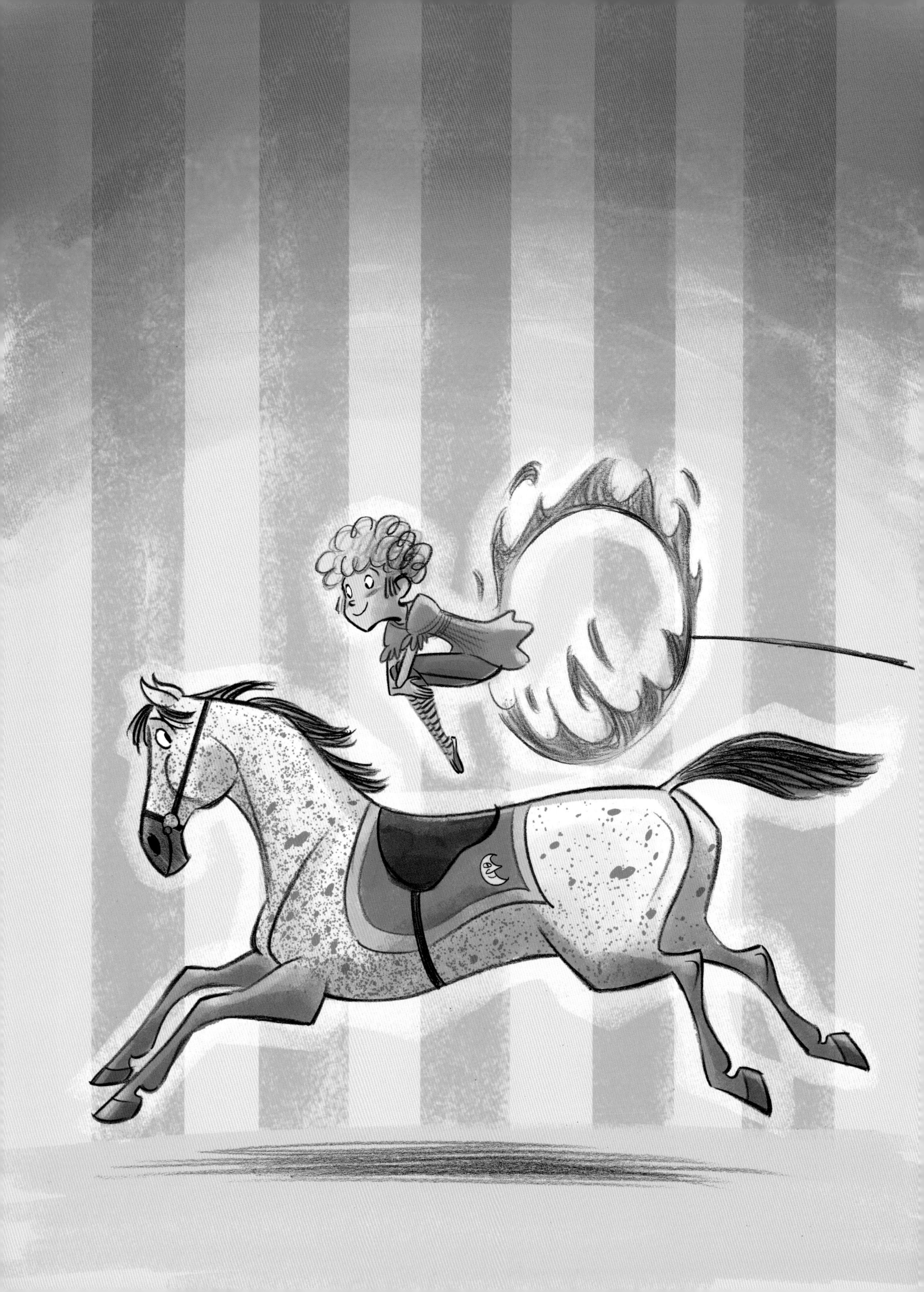

Script:
Teresa Radice

Illustrations and Colors:
Stefano Turconi

Translation by Terrence Chamberlain   Edited by Dean Mullaney

Text and illustrations © 2013 Teresa Radice - Stefano Turconi - Tunué.
Originally published in Italy as *Viola giramondo* by Tunué. All rights reserved.
Published by arrangement with Mediatoon Licensing/Tunué.
Cover design from the French edition, published by Dargaud.

EuroComics.us

Dean Mullaney, CREATIVE DIRECTOR • Lorraine Turner, ART DIRECTOR

EuroComics is an imprint of IDW Publishing,
a Division of Idea and Design Works, LLC
2765 Truxtun Road, San Diego, CA 92106 • www.idwpublishing.com

Distributed to the book trade by Penguin Random House
Distributed to the comic book trade by Diamond Book Distributors

ISBN: 978-1-68405-431-2 • First Printing, March 2019

IDW Publishing
Chris Ryall, President, Publisher, and Chief Creative Officer
John Barber, Editor-in-Chief
Robbie Robbins, EVP/Sr. Art Director
Cara Morrison, Chief Financial Officer
Matt Ruzicka, Chief Accounting Officer
Anita Frazier, SVP of Sales and Marketing
David Hedgecock, Associate Publisher
Jerry Bennington, VP of New Product Development
Lorelei Bunjes, VP of Digital Services
Justin Eisinger, Editorial Director, Graphic Novels & Collections
Eric Moss, Senior Director, Licensing and Business Development

Ted Adams, IDW Founder

Special thanks to Sophie Castille and Émilie Védis at Mediatoon and Cecilia Raneri at Tunué.

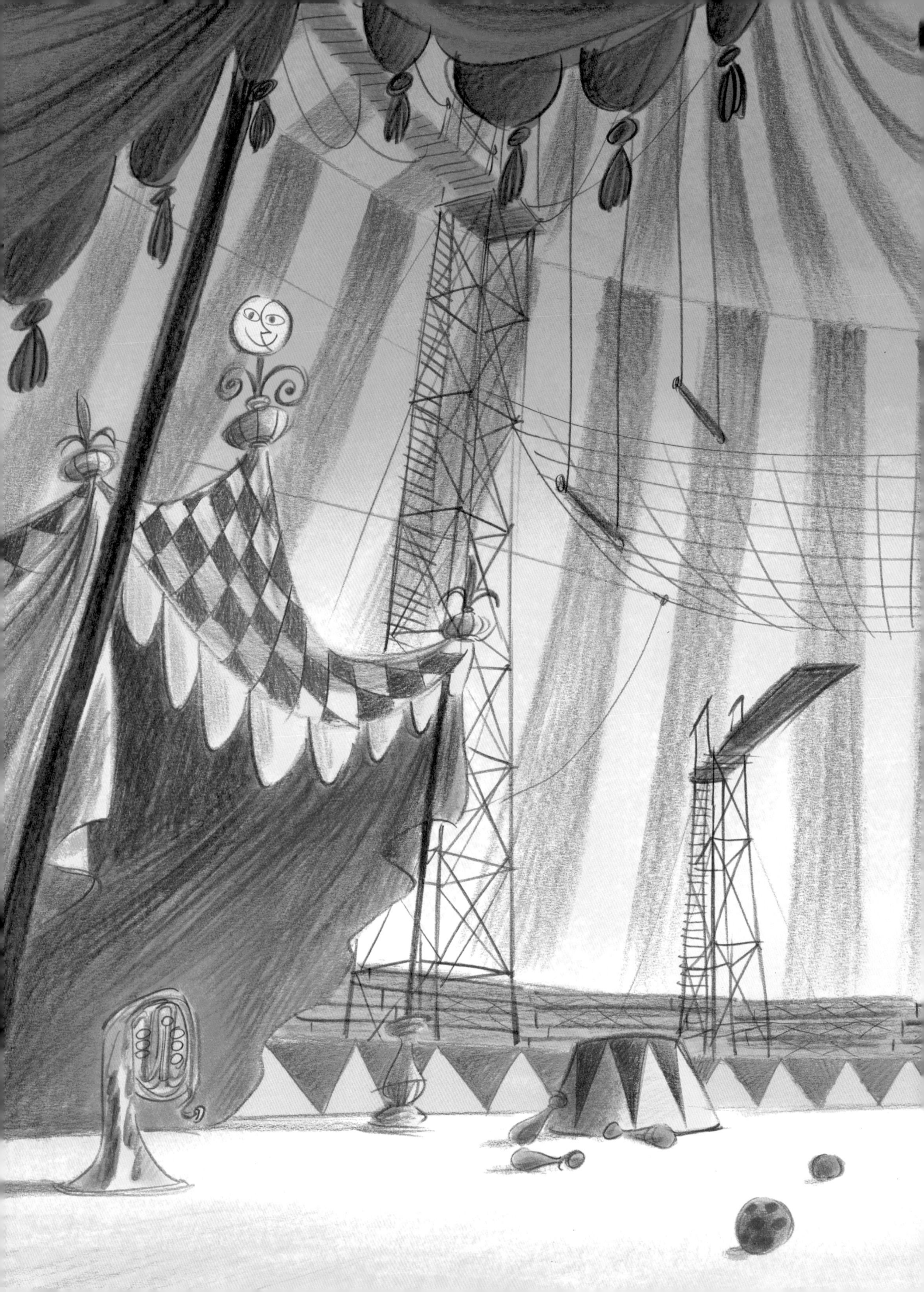